SWIFT
JUSTICE

Other books by Monique Mealue and
*Shane Mealue

Johnny's first job
Johnny goes shopping
Camping trip you will never forget
*Personal vendetta
Short stories you will never forget
*Overcome the hands that's dealt

SWIFT JUSTICE

SHANE MEALUE AND MONIQUE MEALUE

Trafford rev.

 www.trafford.com

North America & international
toll-free: 1 888 232 4444 (USA & Canada)
phone: 250 383 6864 ♦ fax: 812 355 4082

I want to thank God, my husband who co-wrote this book and my son Ray who supported me in writing this book

About the Author:
I live with my husband for twelve years
and Ray in McMinnville, Oregon.

PROLOGUE

Kevin Thomas upon being honorably discharged from serving as an Airborne Ranger in the Vietnam War in 1970 went back to roofing houses. He labored in construction once again for just three months before being accepted in the local police academy.

A well-earned GI loan enables the War Veteran to buy a house with his South Vietnamese wife Linn. It is a two story cottage style home located in Southeast Portland.

The lack of civil law he witnessed firsthand in the cities and villages in Vietnam gave him a mind set to enforce justice so criminals can't do as they please.

June 1971 he begins patrolling Portland Oregon's streets as an eager to serve rookie riding in the passenger side while a superior officer drives.

Having a keen eye for illegal activities on the neighborhood streets along with swiftly taking thugs down quickly gets their attention.

Thomas becomes known on the streets as "Blue Hawk" through many years of aggressively arresting gang members that deal drugs along with violence.

Strife and Strangle Hold is the pair of gangs that have a tight grip on the community with their many illegal activities they do to make money.

Six years of long hours patrolling as well as dangerous altercations with criminals earns Officer Thomas the rank of Sergeant.

1977 is not only a change as far as punk music that Hawk can hardly fathom that has cropped up but the more drug dealing punks on his streets!

The street gangs are tired of dealing with Blue Hawk as much as he is with them on a regular basis. Something is about to explode in the Northwest Oregon city.

CHAPTER 1 _____

Waking up in a cold sweat, Kevin's eyes come into focus peering into the early morning dusk in his bedroom. He faintly sees his pretty wife Ling's brown eyes showing concern. She is trying to comfort him while rapidly saying in her native Vietnamese tongue, "It's only a bad dream! Kevin it's only a bad dream!"

Like the numerous times before the petite south East Asian woman sits up in bed, shaking her husband with both hands to wake him from his vivid dream.

In Thomas's unconscious slumber he was back serving as an Army Airborne Ranger fighting in the Vietnam War. He with his platoon was shooting it out with the Vietcong in the dense jungle in of South East Asia near the Cambodian border; it was the day of a fierce fire fight.

"Whoo, honey, that one seemed so real!" Kevin tells his young Vietnamese wife wiping the beads of sweat from his brow with his hand.

The memories of when he lived in the jungle surviving by the code of kill them first. A soldier in battle doesn't want to give the enemy the chance to sneak up to eliminate him or anyone on his side. Combat that he was participating in years earlier still remains deep in the conscious of the Portland Police officer's war stained mind from serving his country.

The haunting dreams occur at least three times a month ending a peaceful night of rest sending Thomas into a panic attack that sometimes prevents him from getting back to sleep.

3

"You need to seek the help of a psychiatrist to ease the scary thoughts that haunt you in your sleep honey!" Mrs. Thomas says to her shaken husband as she sits close to him on the bed that they share. Still feeling upset Linn remains speaking Vietnamese very fast to the man she loves.

"Remember here in an America you need to stay in practice speaking English!"

"Ha ha very funny Kevin! You know darn well my English is perfect! I think you realize that when I become emotional, I wind up speaking Vietnamese rapidly like a maniac." Linn replies back speaking the usual English language that she studied hard for nearly a year to perfect. She spent many hours diligently trying to learn America's dialect upon coming to the United States from Vietnam.

Mrs. Thomas gets up from the bed, turns around at her husband, "Besides my dear husband. Just because I moved several thousands of miles from my country doesn't make me a total different person. Deep down I am still the same old Ling from my small village in South Vietnam."

"I love it when you talk dirty to me! Come on give me a little lovin!"

"No boom boom for you Mr. Thomas you don't have enough time, you need to get ready for work! Go wash your face and shave off those tiny stubbles! While you are getting ready, I'll start the coffee and fix some eggs for us."

"Sure would like that boom boom, but the coffee and eggs sounds mighty good also."

"Another time sweetheart I promise, now get to moving please!" Linn tells him as she pulls back the blankets leaving Kevin lying in his white brief underwear on their queen size mattress that is covered by a baby blue sheet.

"Hey at least my horrible dreams are like my alarm clock honey!" Thomas tells his wife after turning and gazing at the small black metal wind up clock with the round face that's sitting on his night table. The hands read seven minutes until its alarm is too loudly chime to wake him up for work.

Speaking to the down and out bums is a total waste of time for a metropolitan police officer that patrols the streets. They either find a different spot, but many times a homeless person will walk around the block waiting for you to leave the vicinity.

Once the cop is out of site, the street person or persons again plop themselves right back down in the same spot they desire to routinely occupy.

Pulling into his police station on Alberta Boulevard the rain is coming down a little lighter now, just a mist that forms tiny beads of water on the cruiser's windshield.

Thomas parks in the empty space that is beside his good friend Sergeant Leroy Walker's number 15 squad car. Walker made the rank of Sergeant four months preceding Kevin earning his position as a three chevron Sergeant at the 341st NE precinct 162nd Portland police department.

Leroy is a dark complected black man who is right at six feet tall with a muscular built, who was a star short stop when he went to Lincoln High School.

They have known each other for a handful of years, the pair have gone fishing as well as hunting elk in the Cascade Mountains on a couple of occasions.

Kevin puts on his large dark blue eight point police issued hat with the shiny black plastic bill. It is covered with transparent plastic to keep the rain off the fabric; he adjusts the cap on his head before getting out his number 12 vehicle.

"Good morning Walker, have you shot any bad guys this morning?" Kevin says to his fellow officer peering over the roof of his black and white cruiser after shutting the driver's side door.

"Not yet Thomas, shit it is still early in the day though!" Leroy replies back before closing his vehicle's door with a firm motion.

The two men chuckle as they walk around towards each other to begin casually strolling to the police station entrance together.

"You ready for another exciting meeting this fine day brother?"

"Hell you know me Sgt. Walker I'm always up for a talking to from our beloved Captain!"

Entering the north side station, Sgt. Thomas notices walking down at the other end of the long wide hallway is Deputy Davidson.

His young partner on the force is going in the opposite direction with his back to him. "Hey where ya headed rookie?" He hollers out jokingly knowing good and well that Gary is making his way to the upstairs briefing!

"Good morning Sergeant Thomas, I was just making my way to the little get together that Captain Nicklaus wants to commence by zero six hundred." Davidson informs him as he stops for his superior on the shiny waxed white tile floor of the hall that receives a great amount of foot traffic.

"Well my good deputy I think that I will stroll on up to the second floor meeting area with you to find out what exactly Nicklaus has to inform us all!"

"Probably going to give us the low down on the recent crimes that are committed in our district," Davidson said as he walks beside Thomas up the flight of stairs.

Inside the big briefing room the police officers are seated behind long fold up tables in three rows. They are sitting on thin padded chrome metal framed chairs in front of a wooden podium that is on a raised platform.

One minute before six am, the tall stocky Captain Fred Nicklaus enters the meeting area with a wooden clipboard full of notes gripped in his left hand.

His head is completely shaved bald and he has a neatly groomed dark grey mustache that stops at the corners of his rugged mouth.

Fred was a United States Marine Corps paratrooper in World War 2; he was an able bodied Staff Sergeant that led a platoon through battles in Germany.

He stands behind his usual painted black wood podium with the large Portland police bureau sticker that is sharply displayed on the front of it.

341st's second in command is standing directly front and center of his subordinate audience that is required to intently listen to him as well as take notes on small notebook pads.

"First of all good morning officers, anyway I'll get to the business at hand! I want you all to be on the lookout for a couple of stolen vehicles that have recently been nabbed from citizens here on the north end of town!" The captain says speaking with a slight southern accent.

Men and women cops begin quickly jotting down what Nicklaus is saying using their ink pens. "Car number one is a nineteen sixty eight four door Oldsmobile Sedan light blue in color. Its Oregon plates read Bravo, Charlie, Alpha, seven, five, seven.

"Who reported the grand theft auto the time of the crime Captain Nicklaus? Officer Nadine Farley inquired pausing from taking down her superior's information.

"The victim's next door neighbor reported the crime; unfortunately he didn't see what the perpetrator looked like that night under the dim street light."

Car number two is a grey vinyl top black nineteen seventy two Ford LTD four door sedan. License plates on the Ford read Echo, Alpha, Bravo, four, One, Three with noticeable expired tags."

"Having bad tags is going to make it that much easier to spot the stolen vehicle sir!" Officer Ben Cash blurted out.

"Where exactly was the Oldsmobile taken from Captain?" Sergeant Thomas asked thinking he may have seen it the other day while on duty.

The olds was stolen from 4314 NE Maple Drive two blocks off of Killingsworth Street. This area is known as the Strife gang's territory here on the north side of Portland as you all are aware of officers! A few blocks further away to the east is the newer rival gang to strife called stranglehold."

"Doesn't the strife and strangle hold usually deal with crack cocaine, heroin and prostitution in their large portion of territory?"

"You're probably right Davidson, but I'm not saying that we have any proof that the gangs had anything to do with either automobile. Just beware if they happen to have been involved, the members may be armed and dangerous riding around our city streets!" Captain Nicklaus shows a serious look on his face as he warns the group of police officers from behind his tall wooden stand.

"Most of us remember the time Sergeant Thomas had a shootout with William Bloodgood when he was trying to flee from holding up a small convenience store!"

"Shooting the perpetrator once in the upper left leg and one shot to the dirt bags right wrist, causing him to drop the snub nose thirty eight to the asphalt two years ago."

"Didn't you put that dangerous criminal into the state penitentiary for at least fifteen years?" Walker inquired looking back to where Kevin is sitting.

"Yes, I did! Not only was he a member of the Strife gang, he is also the older brother of the current leader Jimmy Bloodgood."

"You should keep your eye out for him Thomas; he may be gunning for you!" Officer Linda Hayes said a couple chairs over from him.

"I will keep an eye out for Bloodgood so I get the chance to put him away with his big brother so they both can rot in prison together!"

"Jimmy needs to watch out for the rapid firing he may receive from Sergeant Thomas if the punk pulls out a piece!" Shouts out Lieutenant Murdock from two rows back from Kevin.

"You're probably right he is a damn accurate with his Colt forty five automatic!" Nicklaus declares.

162nd Division's Captain double checks his notes to see if there is anything else that needs to be mentioned previously in his address. After noticing nothing else written down he concluded by saying, "That's all I have to say to you this morning officers. Stay alert out there so we can take some of these menacing hoods out of the community the decent citizens live within! Good luck out there this week!" Nicklaus says to his men and women in uniform as they stand up and commence to leave the large meeting room.

Kevin and his partner put on their eight point police hats before exiting the department's building to face the northwest fall rain.

Large cold droplets are now steadily coming down on the early Monday morning in the middle of October while the two men walk toward their patrol car.

Both cops remove their long black night sticks prior to hopping onto the vinyl seat and shutting the car doors almost the same time.

"My friend not only is it our job, it is a way of life buddy boy!" Thomas says as he turns looking at his rookie, uttering in advance of turning the key in the steering column.

"If you say so Sergeant!" Deputy Davidson replies knowing that his superior has a sarcastic wit since riding with the man for a period of over six months.

CHAPTER 2 _____

A week after the briefing with Captain Nicklaus about the couple of full size cars that were ripped off, Kevin is thinking about the neighborhood theft. He is in thought while driving his partner out of the police station's parking lot.

As Sergeant Thomas makes a right hand turn onto the city street, the pair officially begins another day on patrol. "Keep your eyes peeled for anything that looks suspicious deputy and don't forget about the two stolen vehicles." Kevin says.

"Will do Sergeant, but I'm no blue hawk or nothin!" Davidson says giving his partner a hard time by throwing out Kevin's street name of blue hawk.

The blue is because of his uniform's color and the hawk part is that he has the eyes of a predatory bird when it comes to spotting a criminal that is breaking the law.

After hearing it so many times out of the mouths of the law breakers he arrests Thomas puts his foot down speaking up, "Ok that's enough already with the blue hawk! I hear it enough when I come in contact with the punks that hang out on the neighborhood blocks."

"I'm sorry Sergeant; I really didn't mean to piss you off! How long have they been calling you the nick name anyway?" Gary asks looking over sheepishly as he inquires about the unwanted title.

"Coming up on three years now and I still find it a bit annoying to be addressed as a cartoon sounding blue hawk especially by the hard core thugs."

"Hit the lights along with the sirens Davidson!"

"What is it Sergeant?"

"A small orange Datsun hatch back up ahead ran a red light at the four way intersection. If you hadn't been asking me a dumb question, you might have actually witness the illegal move yourself goofball."

"Very funny!" The young deputy replies then radios out to dispatch the 11-95 routine traffic stop.

"Copy that officer over!" Dispatch Amy Henner responds through the speaker.

"Orange Datsun hatchback Oregon plates Echo, Delta, Alpha, One, Six, Two copy that?"

"That's affirmative; I will run a back ground check Deputy Davidson over."

Obeying the signals, the small foreign car begins pulling over to the graveled shoulder of the road. Sergeant Thomas parks the black and white Chevrolet Caprice a distance of about fifteen feet behind the compact vehicle.

Kevin goes to the driver's door, while his young partner goes to the passenger side looking in for anything that appears suspicious.

When the interior seems safe having a single occupant inside the deputy strolls back to the patrol car. Sitting in the passenger seat Davidson picks up the CB radio's mic to find out what is known about the car in front of him.

While waiting for a response from the operator, Kevin gets the driver his licenses then walked back to the patrol car to see if the man behind the wheel has any warrants or anything.

Henner radios back after a brief moment of silence saying, "The vehicle as well as the driver has a clean record."

Sergeant Thomas walks to the driver's rolled down window handing the man his driver's license and registration along with a citation for failure to stop. "Have a nice day sir!" He tells the driver while standing in the drizzly weather. Angrily the man murmurs something under his breath prior to driving the older car away.

"I don't know what that fella is so mad for, Heck I'm the one that is wet from standing in the darn rain!" He light heartedly says to Gary before he sits back behind the wheel of the cruiser.

"Some folks take it personal upon being fined by the men in blue boss!" Davidson replies back showing his grin following his wise ass comment from the passenger side.

While eating at a local mom and pop café, Kevin is looking around the cozy room seeing that that there is a bunch of old memorabilia on the walls.

Covering almost every square inch of the tan painted surfaces are pictures of 1950's rock and roll celebrities along with signed record slicks. Old toys are on shelves that are high up towards the ceiling on each wall for customers to gaze up at while they are eating.

Thomas is casually looking across the room at an old black and white photograph of the king of rock n roll, when he hears, "So how's your wife's leather business doing?"

"Man, I'll tell ya! She has become so busy making woman's purses alone not to mention men's wallets, belts and other accessories. Linn's shop got so busy within a year and half time that she has hired three employees to fill all the orders that come in to her!"

"Does your wife have a star craft worker that she really leans on to get things done Sergeant?"

"There is this long haired hippy dude in his early twenties; at first sight of him I thought he might be a total idiot. Later I discovered that when it comes to leather goods the kid is top notch!"

"What's the guy's name?"

"The kid's name is Glenn, this fella got Linn working with him making leather jackets and vests in her small downtown business location."

"What kind of leather jackets?" Davidson asks staring with a bewildered expression at Sergeant Thomas from the other side of the table.

"Mainly black leather motorcycle rider jackets, although he showed me pictures in his portfolio album of brown suede jackets that I could picture myself wearing to dinner."

"Sounds like Glenn could do about any style a person can request boss."

"He can do about anything you want!" Kevin said as the heavy set waitress set their burger and fries down on the booth's table top in front of them.

"You're not intimidated by Linn making a lot of money by being a powerful career business woman?" Deputy Davidson inquires prior to eating a couple of French fries.

"Not at all, I am proud of my wife for being successful at what she enjoys doing by making leather products!" Sergeant Thomas expressed after swallowing a bite out of his hamburger.

"What about you boss, do you enjoy having to deal with all the dirt bags that sell dope on our city sidewalks?"

"Yes I do! I truly believe men like ourselves are well needed in the community of this fine city. For me the pleasure is putting the bad guys in jail as well as taking their illegal drugs from them before placing them under arrest!"

"I see your point!"

"Enough about my life Gary, what I want to know is when you are going to marry that pretty young girlfriend of yours?" Kevin asks taking the last bite out of his thick burger while staring at the younger man.

Davidson face flushes from his Sergeant's point blank personal question. "Well, I haven't given it much thought when it comes to marrying my girlfriend Janet." He nervously answers back, wishing he didn't have to respond.

"Don't worry about it; you're still a young man friend. I'm just busting your balls a little!"

"You're not a great deal older than I am! when did you and your wife seal the deal?"

"I got married to Linn when I was only nineteen because I am an old fashioned soul that firmly believes in commitment. Plus I absolutely knew that she was the one I want to spend the rest of my life with rookie."

"At this point in my life, I haven't felt as strong of feelings toward a woman as you have described to get married Sergeant."

"How long have you and Janet been an item?"

"Right now we're coming up on close to a year of dating each other seriously."

"You still have plenty of time to make the step Gary!"

"Man you got that right boss, time is exactly what I will be using up before I tie the knot with the opposite sex!"

The rest of the patrolmen's day consists of a few traffic stops on the north east part of Portland. A handful of the cars Thomas had pulled over matched the two grand theft auto vehicle's profile from Monday morning of the previous week's briefing at the 162nd police department.

Unfortunately none of the hopeful automobiles were the right Oldsmobile or Ford Ltd that were anticipated to be a correct match.

Friday mid-morning Kevin and Gary are cruising by an old dirty wooden fence that has a hangman's noose spray painted on it. The barrier is just one of many objects that are tagged with the stranglehold's symbol that is the neighborhood adjacent to north Lombard Street.

"More and more of those damn noose logo's pop up on resident's fences, not to mention on local business owner's veneer walls!" Davidson points out as they slowly travel by the old weathered beaten tan fence with warped boards that are bowing and splitting throughout the upright structure.

"As disgusting as it is, to me it's a reminder of the criminal element that dwells within the core of our citizens communities." Kevin explains to the younger deputy on his right who is listening to every word.

"Take a gander one block straight ahead Sergeant on the right side of the street!"

Scanning to where the Deputy is pointing out, Thomas observes two scantily dressed young women. They each open a car door on the right side of a large American automobile; the pair is preparing to enter the grey four door sedan.

One is a light complected black woman wearing skin tight blue jeans, flashy gold sequined blouse and red high heel shoes. She climbs into the front passenger side sitting next to the driver of the late sixties Plymouth.

The Shorter female is pale white in her late teens, dressed in a very short blue denim skirt that has clusters of different colors rhinestones on the fabric.

She is wearing a snug fitting pink sweater and a pair of blue sparking stiletto heels on her tiny feet as she goes into the passenger rear side door. Anxiously waiting in the back seat is a young male who motions her to come on in.

"Good eyes Davidson, I'm going to speed up a touch so I don't alarm the driver of the vehicle. Last thing I want to do is create a high speed pursuit in a close quartered residential neighborhood!" Kevin says before stepping a little harder on the accelerator gaining more ground on the dark grey Plymouth Fury.

Gary calls the plate into the dispatcher, a few minutes later, information comes back that the vehicle is not stolen. Thomas drives close enough to have a look at the yellow Oregon licenses plate noticing expired tags.

A pair of obvious hookers along with bad tags from the year before is plenty of probable cause to pull the four door Sedan over to the curb.

Davidson instinctually flicks on the lights and sirens of squad car number 12. Upon putting on the right blinker, the chauffeur of the three other people steers the Fury over to the side of the road obeying the officer's command.

Thomas parks the black and white Caprice fifteen feet behind the automobile full of people leaving the flashing lights on, that are mounted to the roof of the police car.

He goes to the driver's side of the vehicle while his partner attempts to ascertain whether the interior of the motor vehicle is safe or not on the opposite side.

"Do you have any idea why I pulled you over today sir?" The strong smell of marijuana smoke hits him the face as he looks down speaking to the Mexican man with curly black hair that is fairly long in length.

"To tell you the truth I really don't have a clue officer!" The man replies back with a slight Hispanic accent.

"I pulled you over because the tags on your vehicle are expired not to mention the two young ladies are known prostitutes in this area. Sir I'll need your license and registration to the vehicle please."

As the motorist is leaning over reaching toward the glove box, Deputy Davidson shouts over the top of the Plymouth's roof, "There is gun on the front floor board Sergeant!"

"Let me see everybody's hands right now!" Sergeant Thomas yells into the open driver's side window at the top of his lungs, with his forty five gripped in hands pointed at the person who was in control of the Plymouth Fury.

Showing no hesitation all four occupants sitting inside the large Sedan reached toward the sky, showing the palms of their hands for the two cops that have pistols out.

"Driver, please listen to me carefully! Slow and easy open the car door using your right to do so while continuing to display your left hand for me to see!" The Curly hair man cautiously does as Kevin tells him with a frightened look on his face as he performs the task.

Deputy Davidson has the African American street walker with the long thin black braids that make up her hair in the front passenger seat come out using similar firm commands to his superior officer.

After patting down the man who was behind the wheel of the Plymouth, he is placed in the back of the patrol vehicle. Sergeant Thomas tells the driver's passenger, "Gentleman in the back sea slowly climb out while showing me both your hands in plain view."

The teenage male with shoulder length brown hair casually exits the left rear door. Kevin swiftly turns the thin built young man around then firmly pats him down from top to bottom feeling for weapons or illegal drugs.

While frisking him, Thomas finds a plastic baggy with a quarter of an ounce of pot and a short brass pipe that is still a little warm to the touch. "You have earned yourself a possession charge." He tells the kid while handcuffing the drug user's hands behind his back while the transparent bag of weed is resting on the Fury's trunk beside him.

"Oh man, give me a break here officer!"

"I'm just detaining you. I have not placed you under arrest yet!" The Sergeant places Scott Andrew the other male with his buddy Ricky Martinez.

Gary is asking the prostitutes for their ID's, when his boss walks up then stands beside him, "I recognize you gals, but we're going to have to see your identifications." Thomas tells them.

A cool shower once again lightly comes down from the dark rain clouds in the sky above. Both young ladies reach into their small purses as the two patrolmen watch every move they make as the dig within. The black hooker is the first to present her Oregon driver's license to Kevin.

"Oh yes! Jenny Emory, are you still walking the streets for the Strangle Hold organization?"

"I'm not telling you a damn thing!"

Thomas is handed the bleach blond prostitutes ID card from his partner to his left, "Martina Smith, I remember you from the raid a year ago on Wayne's Yoon's apartment. That seize turned up close to two ounces of black tar heroin, too bad for us Yoon wasn't there that night!"

"Shit Blue Hawk, I don't know what the hell you're talking about! You have me confused with some other chick!"

In his mind the police Sergeant realizes that the fare skinned tramp is lying to his face. "Ms. Smith the word on the streets is that you also deal with Stuart Thorne, Strangle Hold's leader by doing tricks on the streets to support the neighborhood gang.

"You just heard gossip from rat bastards who make up stuff to save their own skins!"

"Please call these in Davidson, see what you can turn up on these young ladies." Hawk hands his partner the pair of whore's plastic identification cards to radio into the dispatch operator to run a background check.

"Hey Sergeant, what about the pat down search prior transporting them to booking at the station?"

"Hold up a second Davidson, we need a female officer to frisk Ms. Emory and Ms. Smith. District policy changed last month where we are required to use female officers to search the women law breakers!"

"That's right Sir!"

Gary walks to the black and white to request at least one female officer to search the ladies. A few minutes later, Staff Sergeant Kathy Norton responds by saying, "Me and Sergeant Walker will be there in an estimated time of roughly ten minutes over."

Kevin strolls to squad car 12 to see what the status is on additional officers arriving to the scene. Hawk leans into the open passenger door as the deputy hangs up the receiver to the CB radio. "We have Walker in route with Norton to frisk the pair of females; I also was informed that both working girls have outstanding warrants for their arrests."

"Glad to hear that one of our few north side woman cops are on patrol when we need to utilize them for a specific purpose on the street."

"To me it seems pretty ridiculous that we have to take up a woman officer's time to aid in a routine pat down when we could simply do it ourselves." Davidson said as he looks up from the passenger seat.

"Deputy I'm all for it because one time in the past I pat searched a woman in her mid-thirties on a drunk and disorderly call at the Westward bar. She accused me of inappropriately touching her before putting in the back seat of my patrol car in her intoxicated state of mind."

Sergeant Walker parks his number 15 cruiser behind's Kevin's vehicle. He and his partner perambulate up to where the two waiting patrolmen are, "We heard you are in need of a little assistance Sergeant!" Kathy states as she walks up with Leroy to where her fellow officers are at beside their issued Chevy Caprice.

"As you are aware of Sergeant Norton, we can't search the opposite sex before arresting them. So if you would do the honor of performing the task my partner and I can haul in a couple of Johns that have a good size amount of marijuana along with concealed handgun."

"It will be my pleasure to help out in the situation gentlemen!" The tall stocky police woman strides over with her partner then promptly starts frisking the black woman first as Walker watches.

After both women are patted down and handcuffed, they are being led to Walker's patrol vehicle with their hands secured behind their backs.

When the two women of the streets are going by Hawk being led by the two additional officers to their black and white vehicle Martina turns her head to Thomas yelling, "Some people are gunna be seriously pissed off when they find out that we're locked up Blue Hawk!"

Sergeant Thomas doesn't give much thought to what the mouthy hooker spat out. He just walks to his vehicle with Davidson to take the two male subjects to the to book them for possession and with patronizing known prostitutes.

While they are patrolling again following dropping off the two young Johns at their police precinct, Gary looks over at his partner,

"Hey are you worried about what that hooker yelled at you earlier boss?"

"If I sweated everything that is said to me by the people that I arrest on the city streets, I wouldn't have the guts to do this job for a living!" Kevin gazed over to his deputy explaining his sentiments.

CHAPTER 3 ————————————————

Monday evening a little past five that day, Kevin as usual is dropping off his younger partner off at their 162nd division police station. "I will see you tomorrow morning for another day to catch bad guys." The Portland police sergeant says to Deputy Davidson just prior to him stepping out the passenger door to find his car.

At his humble home, Thomas grabs a quick bite to eat to get him by before strolling to his bedroom to change out of his dark blue uniform.

He puts on his much more comfortable black kung Fu clothing along with the black canvas slip on shoes that go with the uniform.

Kevin and Linn have been studying at the "Dragon's Fury Martial Arts Studio on SW Broadway Street in Portland for over four years. They have both earned brown sashes, which are the equivalent to brown belts in karate.

The two of them take private lessons together Monday, Wednesday and Friday six to seven thirty with their Chinese American instructor Charles Lee. They have a long way to go before they can take their test to earn the black sashes on their uniforms.

That cool damp evening the Thomas's are first fine tuning their Kung-Fu forms being led by instructor Lee after a long stretch out on the mat.

Charles may be a foot shorter than Kevin but he is every bit as strong as well as being a lot faster in his movements from a life time of dedication to his martial art.

Taking turns sparring against each other for the last forty minutes of class concludes the training for the day. "Remember you two practice every chance you get on perfecting your Kung-Fu capabilities! Always keep in mind to only use the ancient skills I teach you to protect yourselves if harm comes your way!" Lee says before the three of them bow to each other.

"Charlie I've been trying to perfect those free flowing moves you showed me a week ago using my police issued night stick!"

"Is what I showed you to do becoming any easier for you Mr. Thomas?"

"Quite a bit smoother along with much greater force in my strikes to the heavy punching bag that I have in the garage at my house."

Upon finishing the sweaty Martial arts lesson, Linn and her husband take a shower in the men's and woman's locker room to freshen up. The hot water soothes Thomas's sore aching muscles that he acquired from having a long tiring day.

After changing into their regular clothes the married couple goes to the Pioneer's kitchen family restaurant a few miles from their urban home.

They have been going there for delicious meals for several years in their busy lives. Most of the time Kevin orders the chicken fried steak he enjoys so much while Linn either has a burger and fries or a Chinese dish.

While waiting for his food that he ordered a few minutes previously, Kevin catches himself nodding off to dream land sitting on the soft cushioned seat.

"Wake up Mr. sleepy man!" Linn playfully says with her strong Asian accent as she touches her husband's hand that is resting palm down on the table.

"Sorry honey it's been a long day for me. I will try to keep my heavy eyes lids open, so I won't pass out with my face buried in a plate of mashed potatoes and gravy!"

Mrs. Thomas laughs at picturing what he would look like drowning in his own food. "Kevin that would be a site to see, with you I can see the occurrence happening sweetheart!" He starts chuckling; rubbing his eyes tired dried eyes with his thick fingers.

Casually the loving couple enjoys each other's company sharing their thoughts all throughout their hot dinners at the fine dining establishment.

Later that night at home shortly before nine thirty, Kevin finishes brushing his teeth in preparation for a needed night of sleep to ready himself for another day.

While his beautiful petite wife lies on the bed watching him, the police sergeant sluggishly pulls off the red cotton t-shirt then removes his blue jeans placing them into a drawer.

Upon lying under the covers next to his wife he tells Linn he loves her and wishes the loving woman pleasant dreams. In no time at all Thomas falls into a deep slumber promptly after uttering the few words to his spouse.

The next few days of patrolling are routine, what most patrolmen might consider uneventful as far as action in the line of in police duty.

Friday morning is a dark overcast day that has the appearance that it could rain at any moment in a heavy down pour.

Thomas and Davidson are driving down, what is considered Strife's turf right around a quarter past ten am making their presents known as they look for illegal activity.

Kevin spots a suspicious vehicle and what he recognizes as two young males standing beside a large four door Sedan. It appears to him to be the act of a drug deal in the middle of a pothole filled graveled alley.

"Man, if those fellas don't look like they're up to no good Sergeant!"

"Sure appears to be the making of a shady deal going down before our eyes. I'm rotating us around the block Deputy to come up in front of them, to cut them off at the pass!"

"I better call in back up because they might be some salty dudes that will do something stupid boss!"

"Make it quick Davidson, I have a funny feeling that our perpetrators will try to make a run for it."

Gary gives Thomas a quick understanding nod as he picks up the CB's black plastic mic. "This is car twelve; please send back up to our location. We are checking a suspicious vehicle in an alley between sixteen and market over."

"Rodger that! I'm sending patrol car fifteen to assist in the matter."

"Thank you, over and out!" Davidson says.

Kevin cruises his squad car slowly into the narrow alleyway that is lined with wood fences and the back sides of commercial cinderblock buildings.

He remembers the plate number on the large metallic red Oldsmobile to be one of the stolen vehicles that was mentioned at the briefing.

A shaggy haired male that's behind the car's steering wheel glances up viewing the approaching black and white cruiser closing in on him.

Without any haste, the punk places the car in reverse and steps down hard on the vehicle's accelerator sending gravel flying from the spinning rear tires. The teenage boys that are outside the Oldsmobile dart off climbing over a home owner's graffiti covered wood fence.

Deputy Davidson jumps out of patrol car twelve while Sergeant Thomas briefly brings the automobile to a stop. He rushes to grab his long black nightstick prior to slamming the passenger door behind him.

Gary sprints to the entrance they came in to circle around the block to cut off the juveniles with his belly club tightly gripped in his right hand.

Kevin is in pursuit of the blue Sedan that is speeding off in reverse with two subjects that are attempting to elude capture from justice.

Brown muddy water is splashing out of the deep mud puddles in huge wakes as the Oldsmobile hurries across the rough road at a high rate.

They're going into the many large divots on the alley's unkempt street sending water flying as well as steam into the cold morning air.

"Damn, you stupid son of a bitch," Kevin says out loud at the driver of the other vehicle as the criminal backs out to the left onto the through the street.

He came within inches of nearly hitting an oncoming car that has a little boy in the passenger seat riding next to his mother as she takes him to school.

Not even glancing back for a second, the street hood slaps the vehicle in drive then hurries down the neighborhood streets at a fast rate not caring about the consequences.

The other cars on the road are doing their best to get out the way of the maniac that is operating the large American automobile.

"This is Sergeant Thomas, I'm pursuing a blue nineteen sixty eight Oldsmobile Delta 88', the plates read Bravo, Charlie, Alpha, seven, five, seven. This is one of the vehicles that were recently stolen from the north east side of town."

"What is the location of the subjects?"

"They have just made a left turn off of fifteenth street, as of now are heading east on Gilburt Avenue speeding towards NE 37th street." Kevin radios in while he is three cars lengths behind the pair of careless law breakers.

"This is Lieutenant Gronich with staff Sergeant Colvin in patrol car fifteen, the suspects are coming toward us!" He says in a strong Mexican accent riding shot gun as his partner rapidly drives with the lights and sirens on.

"I read you loud and clear Lieutenant!"

"We are going to pull over on a side street out of site then lay out a set of spike strips on Gilburt Avenue, so beware Thomas over and out!"

Kevin hangs up the mic, continuing to chase after the metallic blue Sedan while commuters pull over to the side of the road letting him pass when they see his flashing lights.

He slows down when he sees the spikes that the perpetrators have just run over up ahead of him.

The last thing Hawk needs is to have flat tires trying to catch a couple of drug dealing thugs in a high speed pursuit. Red haired Tom Colvin quickly drags the three foot strip of spikes off of the asphalt allowing his fellow officer to pass.

Though two of the Oldsmobile's tires are deflated to almost completely flat, the panicking dope peddler keeps giving it everything the car has to continue fleeing. Thomas goes behind the vehicle to perform a pit maneuver to try to end the chase once and for all.

Acting as if he were going to pass the blue Sedan on the left side, the Portland police Sergeant gets on the rear side of the Olds then cranks his steering wheel hard to the right.

Patrol car twelve's chrome front bumper strikes the opposing vehicle with great force in the rear quarter panel. It is a hard hitting impact sends the other automobile traveling into a one eighty about face skid.

The Oldsmobile Delta 88' slides on the wet surface of the black top to the left so fast and hard it jumps the concrete curb ending up in a fairly deep ditch.

Steam is bellowing out from under the overheated Old's hood as the disabled vehicle sits sideways partially resting in shallow water. Kevin is fast to pull up to the Delta 88', while squad car fifteen is arriving right behind him.

By the time Hawk brings his issued vehicle to a complete stop the tall muscular black man with the Hendrix style hair who was driving is already fleeing the scene.

He is running in a wide open grassy field that is on the other side of the water filled culvert. His accomplice is injured not moving as he remains seated on the passenger side of the disabled four door Sedan.

When Thomas got out of patrol car number twelve, he forgot to grab his handy night stick that was leaning in the middle area of the front bench seat.

"Take the suspect that is in the vehicle, you may have to radio for an ambulance!" Kevin yells out just before going into a mad dash after the drug dealer that's in the process of making a getaway.

Colvin and Gronich drew their pistols on the perpetrator that's still in the Oldsmobile, "Get out with your hands where we can see them now!"

There is no response from the passenger due to having his head bounce off the vehicle's dashboard knocking him unconscious. He has a two inch gash above his right eyebrow that is weeping dark red blood down his closed eye.

"Halt now!" Hawk hollers out with ferocity at the suspect who is around sixty feet from him now as he begins to slightly slowdown from fatigue.

"Kiss my ass pig!" The culprit yells over his shoulder in between heavy breaths while running as fast as he can get his tired legs to move.

Glancing back while on the move, the African American perpetrator attempts to see how far back the trailing police man is behind him.

He trips over a small tree limb that is lying on the soft saturated grass from not paying attention to what is in front of his feet.

Scurrying to get back up again to sprint away, the dealer is only able to take a couple of steps when Sergeant Thomas tackles him from behind knocking him flat onto his stomach.

In the quickness Hawk has the suspect's left arm behind his back. He places the strong black guy's left hand in a painful joint lock sending pain to the pressure point that is in the subject's wrist joint.

An insubordinate hostile street wise punk flails about fighting back with his free right hand as Kevin tries to place the handcuffs on the suspect's wrists.

"Stop resisting arrest and give me your other hand! You can do this the easy way or the hard way! It is totally up to you right now!" "Sergeant Thomas bends down even harder on the perpetrator's bent back hand causing a lot more pain in the pressure point area.

"AAHH! AAHH! You're gunna break my damn arm pig!" The bad guy shouted out before having no choice but to give up his right arm so Kevin could handcuff both of his wrists behind his back.

After cuffing the black male, Hawk notices a tattoo of an "S" with a dagger going down through it on the back of his hand in the location between his thumb and fore finger.

The light complected skin tone hood unbeknownst to Thomas is Tyrese Jackson the number two man in the strife street gang.

All he knew by the tattoo is that this is one of the punk asses who likes to break many ordained laws that he is hired to enforce while on duty.

He swore an oath with one hand on the King James Bible to uphold justice in the state of Oregon. A lawbreaker is to be captured in the same manner no matter if you're the number one gang member or considered the lowest man.

They are all the same to Kevin, equally all worthless when it comes to being in a normal society that he loves within the northwest city he grew up in.

Sergeant Thomas is walking the hoodlum that has mud all over the front of his faded blue denim jacket and pants. He has his hands tightly cuffed behind his back as he is being lead to the number twelve squad car.

"You and your fuzzy buddies' aint got nuthin on us blue Hawk!" The number two gang member chuckles defiantly following his remark.

"We'll see about that here in a matter of minutes. Those two officers over there will find anything illegal hidden within the stolen vehicle you were operating. Watch your head Mr. Jackson!" Thomas tells Tyrese as he helps him into the back seat of his black and white Caprice.

Tyreses's accomplice is in the back seat of patrol car fifteen holding a small white towel to his head to help stop the bleeding.

Staff Sergeant and Lieutenant Gronich diligently search the large Oldsmobile Sedan to see if there is any unlawful contraband stashed within the interior of the car.

Under the front seat, one of the police officers found a good size transparent plastic zip lock bag full of individually packaged and sealed small baggies of crack cocaine. They also found a black single action three fifty seven magnum with a six inch barrel. The handgun's serial numbers were ground off giving it the appearance of a stolen weapon.

"You boys roll big don't you fella!" Colvin states as he holds up the items were found in front of the suspect seated in his squad car with the door open.

Lieutenant Gronich ambulates over to where Kevin is standing beside his vehicle, "Me and my partner found some more reasons why these two fled like a couple of crazy people other than just a stolen vehicle charge."

"What all did you find Lieutenant?"

"We pulled out close to two ounces of crack that is ready to be sold to customers on the street as well as what I believe is an illegal pistol."

"I'll tell you what, someone much bigger than these two small time punks are not going to be too happy about the bust that is happening here today! Thomas states.

"Maybe they'll take the message that they might be in the wrong line of work and move on!"

"Wouldn't that be nice if that were to only happen but it's very doubtful to actually take place. Have you heard if the other two subjects that were fleeing on foot were apprehended?" Kevin asks.

"I found out from dispatch a little while ago that Deputy Davidson was picked up by Sergeant Walker. He was taken to the station with a young suspect that he brought into custody after a foot chase."

"How is the passenger from the Oldsmobile doing Lieutenant Gronich?"

"Marvin Jones has a cut on his forehead that might require a few stitches. He will be transported to the hospital by ambulance prior to being booked."

"Very well then, I will see you at the station; I've got some paperwork to get started on these jokers!" Sergeant Thomas says then quickly turns around getting into his number twelve patrol car sitting behind the wheel.

"You think you and the other uniformed fuzz can stop the dope that is brought into this city to be sold, Blue Hawk!" Tyrese defiantly states sitting directly behind Kevin with his hands cuffed tightly behind his back.

The Portland police Sergeant peers into the Chevrolet's rear view mirror to look upon the dark skinned man, who is loudly speaking.

"So your saying that law enforcement doesn't have a chance at changing things on the neighborhood streets Mr. Jackson or should I calls you Black Mamba?" Thomas said just before putting the car in drive cruising away from the scene.

"My name is not important I am just one of the many men that make a link in a powerful chain! One last thing Blue Hawk before I used my right to remain silent, the streets are a civil battle field. The police are facing a war that is set up for the resistance to dominate society!"

CHAPTER 4 _____

It is the third week in November; around five thirty in the evening. After setting up the table for dinner, Kevin sits down with Linn eating spaghetti with French bread at their dining room table. "Honey, I think you should sign up for those classes on forensic medicine and criminal investigation at the community college." Linn mentions before taking another bite of food off her fork.

"I don't know if I have time in my busy schedule that I currently have my dear."

"Remember telling me the times you showed up first at the scene of a homicide. You told me you felt helpless from not being able to do much only putting up the yellow plastic barrier tape around the perimeter of the murder site."

"I recall complaining about feeling like an idiot having to observe at a distance while the detectives worked on solving the crime."

"Honey please sign up, they begin in January. I think you can easily attend semester classes at Lewiston Community College. Plus there are full day courses on Saturday and Sunday as far as I read. They cater to the police officers that want to advance to the detective rank in Law enforcement." Linn explains.

"Sounds like you did a little investigating of you own!" Kevin said subsequent to taking a bite of spaghetti from the heap on his large white dinner plate.

"Yes sweetheart I did! The time is right because we have the money to pay for it finally."

"Well dear, I can't argue too much with that Linn especially since our savings account is fat with money."

The following week on a Tuesday, while Kevin is having a lunch break, he commutes to Lewiston Community college in the neighboring town of Gladstone. His classes, if everything goes ok will begin Saturday January fifth at eight o clock in the morning.

Thomas felt that he is taking a step in the right direction as he filled out several enrollment forms in the admission office at the college.

"Detective Kevin Thomas the title has an air of importance to it if I do say so myself." A brief random thought crosses his mind while writing down his information using a black ball point pen on the multi question forms.

The next day while patrolling their beat, Kevin is smiling from ear to ear, when Davidson comments, "What are you grinning about boss? Did you get laid last night or something?"

"Ya, we got it on last night, but that's not what I'm smiling about. Yesterday on your day off, I enrolled at Lewsiton community college in the studies of Forensic science and criminal investigation!"

"That's awesome Sergeant, you're going to work at advancing yourself to Detective!"

"I have thought about doing it for quite a while now Deputy, for one reason or another but didn't take the initiative to get the process underway."

"You are due for advancement in rank Thomas."

"Thank you Gary!"

While they were chit chatting through the early morning boredom a call came in from dispatch from the other end of the CB radio, "Car twelve please come in over!"

"This is Deputy Davidson of car twelve over."

"There is a 459 in progress at thirty second and Lombard Street at Mark's pharmacy."

"Copy that, we are in route to the scene over and out."

Kevin turns on the lights and siren to have the commuter's pull off to the shoulder of the road, so he could speed to the large pharmaceutical business. A silent alarm at the commercial drug store alerted the police station of the break in that is in progress.

On the way to the crime scene, Kevin pulls back his long sleeve shirt navy blue cuff. He notices that it is eight minutes to nine. "The pharmacy isn't open yet, so I'm thinking that the perpetrator or perpetrators broke in from the back of the building. Thomas says.

"That's more than likely what occurred." Davidson replies looking over at his superior.

The squad car's tires make a loud high pitch screech sound as it driven around a sharp corner at a fairly fast rate of speed turning to the right. A small Japanese pick up and station wagon pulled over to the shoulder when they hear the police vehicle's loud siren blaring.

Deputy Davidson flicks off the roof lights and siren four blocks from Mark's pharmacy to avoid drawing attention to themselves by the criminals.

A few blocks from the business Hawk stops the number twelve squad car. Before getting out of the Caprice Kevin tells his subordinate partner, "I'm going to sneak around to the back of the store to try to get a jump on them!"

"I will keep my eyes peeled just in case you wind up flushing them out the front doors!"

"Be careful Davidson! Try to utilize a place you can take cover behind in case things become hectic!"

The rookie grabs his night stick from the interior of the Chevrolet then slowly jogs in the direction of the front side of pharmacy.

Hawk cruises the police vehicle cautiously to the alley behind the medical business. Up ahead close to the rear entrance the Portland Police officer views the perpetrator's beat up yellow Volkswagen bug.

Clearly Thomas can see that there is no one inside of the small German car. He quietly parks within thirty feet of the kicked in grey solid metal door.

Calmly Thomas opens the cruiser's driver's side door in a manner to be as inaudible as possible. Once standing on the black top Kevin quickly unsnaps the metal button on his handgun's black leather holster.

In one swift upward movement Hawk has his blued colt forty five automatic pistol firmly gripped in his powerful right hand. He flicks the safety switch off then double checks to ensure there is a round in the chamber before sneaking to where the forced entrance occurred.

Lickety split Kevin is on the hinge side of the door jam with his back to the cold green painted cinder block wall with his gun pointed to the ground. Carefully he pushes the sheet metal door that is slightly cracked open six inches.

The door hinges made a noisy creaking sound when Thomas pushed through quickly that he wished wouldn't have happened.

Rapidly he crouches down and hurries to the left taking a knee upon entering the poorly lit storage room of the pharmaceutical retail store.

Out of the blue the police Sergeant hears the deafening sound of a gunshot that sends a bullet whizzing over his head from in front of him.

It is from a thin Caucasian man who saw the cop then dropped the small cardboard box of pills he was carrying to their vehicle.

The pale complicated perpetrator with red stubbly facial hair wasted no time drawing out his revolver when he came into the room and caught sight of the cop.

Without hesitation Kevin returns fire sending a forty five caliber slug into the chest of the druggie that is trying to end his life.

Hawk's center mass shot sent the criminal flying backwards off his feet. He ended up flat on his back on the smooth glossy finish of the cold concrete floor. The low life's snub nose revolver is still tightly gripped in his hand as he lies motionless starring up at the ceiling eyes wide open.

Advancing forward taking cover on the right side of the open doorway where the perpetrator is laying lifeless beside a stack of cardboard boxes.

Kevin observes the top of two heads on the opposite side of the cashier area of the couple of suspects that are ducked down.

"This is Sergeant Thomas of the northeast Portland police bureau! I want you both to put down your weapons and come toward me slowly with your hands raised high above your heads!" He yells at the two criminals with his back resting against the painted cinder block wall having the side of his head to the door jamb.

Following Thomas's direct order there was a barrage of gun fire from over the top of the wide check stand. Instinctively Kevin ducked back from the deadly line of fire that is rapidly being laid down.

When the burglars finish shooting in the police Sergeant's direction, they waste no time taking cover once again. Hawk pivots out then quickly fires six rounds into the tall wood counter before hurrying to the position he spun out from.

Back against the thick inner wall of the building, Thomas slaps a full clip into the colt then pulls the slide back placing another live bullet in the chamber.

Thomas peers around the side of the door jamb viewing a tall skinny black teenager shoot out the front door's glass using a twelve gauge pump shot gun.

Tiny shards of glass fly in an explosive way out side landing on the concrete sidewalk and on the black top in front of the business.

The young criminal desperately rushes out of the opening with a small white plastic garbage bag of pharmaceutical drugs in one hand and the weapon in the other.

Off in the distance, the hollering of Deputy Davidson can be heard inside Mark's Pharmacy prior to a gunshot going off out in the parking lot.

Kevin stepped cautiously over the dead thief that has his mouth open giving him an appearance of surprise on his dirty pale looking face.

He creeps ever so slowly as well as silent making his way the short span to the wooden barrier that has many pull out drawers have a look on the opposite side.

Being fully aware of the one remaining perp; the police Sergeant's forty five automatic is aimed out in front of him as he uses both of his hands to steady the handgun.

Hawk rounds the left side of the counter finding a muscular built black male sitting with his back resting against the structure's front surface.

The neighborhood criminal is holding the blood soaked area of a tight fitting grey tee shirt at his abdominal region of his body.

Wounded grimacing in pain the petty thief has his head turned to the left staring widely in the shadows of the unlit drug store's room.

Though hurting badly he is still gripping his black nine millimeter automatic in his left hand, when Hawk says, "Please toss your weapon away from you now sir! I will radio for medical attention once you have done so. Just get rid of your gun in your hand!"

"I aint goin back to the state pen pig!" A shaky perspiring perpetrator says before slowly raising the pistol in his hand pointing it in the Thomas's direction.

Without hesitation Hawk squeezed the trigger on the forty five he is carefully aiming with his two hands sending a heavy slug through the side of the street punk's skull.

The impact of the shot drove the black man's body lying on its right side on the cold concrete floor in one powerful motion.

Kevin removes the handgun from the dead burglar's hand as his mind couldn't help but think, "You didn't have to do that asshole!"

Slow and cautiously the Police Sergeant walks down a wide isle with the tall shelves on both sides of him that leads to the glass doors of the building's entrance.

He has the pistol from the criminal firmly grasped in his right hand pointed at the at the white and black tile floor. Hawk looks left and right scanning the room as he exits the building's premises.

As he begins to come out of the broken out opening, Thomas views Sergeant Walker along with Staff Sergeant Norton. Both police officers are taking cover behind their wide open front doors of their assigned patrol car that's front end is facing toward the front of the business.

"Hey gentlemen it's Sergeant Thomas, I'm coming out now! Please hold your fire, I'm exiting the pharmacy!"

"Come on out Sergeant, your clear to come forward to us!" Leroy Walker yells back half way across the parking lot from his issued number fifteen Chevy Caprice while feeling relieved to hear his friend and coworkers voice.

While discussing what went down with his fellow officers an ambulance is taking away the injured subject that Davidson was forced to shoot.

Across the street a local news team can be seen reporting what has just transpired to North West viewers at home. A young rookie cop is a close distance from the reporters to keep them at bay from the scene of the crime.

The pair is riding back to the station when Gary exclaims, "Man you took those low life's out in short order this morning! You really showed them not to mess with the men in blue that enforce the law!"

"If I teach you only one thing while you are riding on patrol with me rookie!" Hawk paused momentarily after speaking prior to glancing over to his younger partner.

He takes a calming deep breath before continuing to talk, "Here's how it is Deputy, killing a man isn't something you gloat about afterward. Today I feel sick to my stomach by taking the lives of those two individuals."

"Is it any different killing the bad guys now from back when you fought in the war?"

"In Vietnam they were considered the enemies of the United States; it was a conflict far away in a foreign country. Even though I didn't feel bad about killing enemy soldiers, I still didn't reveal from my actions in combat to anybody!"

"I see your point boss, but you did what you had to do in a difficult situation today!"

"Maybe so Davidson, here in the community I want to bring criminals to justice through the judicial system. "What I'm trying put across is that I wish I could have brought all the burglars in without a single shot being fired."

"It's not your fault how things went, that I do know for sure Sergeant!"

"I appreciate you saying that Deputy!"

Later that afternoon upon finishing filling out the incident report at the police station, Sergeant Thomas is called into Captain Fredrick Nicklaus's office.

Ill at ease Kevin sits on the cushioned chair directly in front of his superior's large desk knowing good and well what he is about to be told.

"I am sorry that I have to do this, but it is department procedure when a police officer uses deadly force by way of utilizing a firearm. You will be required to have a unpaid week off while your deadly use of a side arm is investigated. It doesn't even matter whether the cop appears to be in the right or in the wrong Sergeant Thomas." Nicklaus is leaning forward with his thick hairy forearms resting on the surface of his desk displaying a sincere look in his eyes as he spoke.

"Even though I don't fully agree with being forced to take a leave of absence from my routine duties, I will keep a positive attitude trusting to be fairly treated."

"You have my word Thomas that the fact finding inquisition will be strictly performed by the book with myself along with Chief Blythe."

Kevin stood up after the Captain rose to his feet on the other side of the metal barrier that has several files on top of it. Nicklaus swiftly strolled around and shook Thomas's hand telling him, "All this will be behind very soon!"

"Thank you sir for your words of encouragement." The heavy hearted Portland police Sergeant briskly left the room to head home and begin the unwanted time off.

CHAPTER 5 ————————

On the north east side of Portland, Strangle Hold leader Stuart Thorne is in his run down two bedroom house in his ghetto neighborhood. He is drinking cheap domestic beer with his former gang member Andy Collins who now a member of Strife.

Andy switching gangs never affected the friendship or the way Stuart and him used each other to make money selling illegal drugs.

Collins has brought over Troy Taggerd and Marty Walters two trustable well known pot smokers that live close by to each score an eighth of high grade marijuana.

All of them are taking swigs from their brews while swapping stories of when they were much younger as they sit on rough looking furniture.

A large wood console television set with a twenty five inch screen is playing a mystery drama that no one in the living room pays much attention to.

"Hey dude! I don't mean to spoil the fun but I have to split to pick up my old lady from work!" Marty says as he looks at Collins after noticing what it has become.

"That's cool with me man, I'm going to hang out here and suck down some suds with Stuart for a while longer."

Both guys leave with their thick bags of bud stuffed in the inside pockets of their well-used winter coats to hoof it back to Marty's place.

While they are talking, the evening news began on the channel that is set on the TV. A woman reporter with long straight black hair shows up on the screen. Out of the blue the two gang members began to focus upon what the attractive lady had to say.

She is reporting across the street from Mark's pharmacy holding a red umbrella over her head to block the rain, "Earlier this morning two local gang members by the names of Douglas Ulrich and Warren Washington were killed as they tried to burglarize the family owned business. A quick responding Portland Policeman shot both of the deceased criminals. Tyrell Washington was wounded in the shoulder while fleeing armed coming towards another officer."

"What in the hell is up with this shit! Those were a couple of our best men! I want to know very soon which cop killed them!"

The six foot five, two hundred and ninety pounds man quickly stands up from his lazy boy chair, hurries over to the television. He pushes in the chrome button shutting off the large TV set using way more effort than his necessary.

Thorne looks back to Collins exhibiting his rage, "Find Wayne, I want to find out what he knows on the street about our loss today!" Stuart loudly tells him displaying a bright red face from anger, his green eyes showing how insane his is as gazes around the room.

"I'll put the word out on the street that you want to see him as soon as possible!"

"Do that Yoon is the man that keeps my organization rolling at full force!" Andy swiftly turns leaving the gang leader's small home that is two blocks from Lombard Street.

A couple of days later the number two guy for Strangle Hold shows up at his leader's residence. The Korean immigrant has the answers Stuart is looking for in his mind from the snitches he uses in Portland for answers.

He confidently strolls up the narrow walkway to the shabby beige cottage with the broke down Ford on the over grown lawn.

Lee Valentine a half white; half Chinese thin guy answers the door telling the well-dressed man that has a black belt in Tae Kwon Do, "Come on in, Thorne has been looking forward to speaking with you!"

In the dining room table, Thorne is wearing a tight fitting white tank top shirt that shows off his stocky sleeve tattooed arms.

A menacing appearing career criminal is sitting on the opposite side of a blue dining room table with chrome metal legs. "Please sit down brotha; I have a few things I want to talk to you about my friend!"

"You takeoff for a few Lee, I want to talk to Wayne alone for a bit!" Stuart tells his low life subordinate with a serious look on his face.

"You got it boss!" Valentine says prior to exiting out the beat up front door of the house.

Previous to engaging in the little question and answer session, Thorne breaks out a small mirror along with a transparent plastic bag of crack cocaine. He puts down a couple of thick lines using a well-used razor blade for the two of them to snort up.

Stuart snorts his up first then hands the small mirror across the table to the eagerly awaiting Yoon. Wayne wastes no time snorting up the fat white rail of powder through the rolled up one dollar bill that stuffed into his right nostril.

"Tell me you know the pig that killed our brothers out on the streets the other day!"

"Stuart my eyes and ears that roam this city have told me not only the cop's name but also where his sweet Asian wife has her business." Wayne exclaims showing a cocky expression on his face while doing so.

"Damn it spit it out already man!"

"It's that son of a bitch Blue Hawk or as he is formally known as Sergeant Kevin Thomas!"

"That figures Yoon, the same fuzz that's been giving us trouble in our business for years did this!"

Suddenly a firm knock on the door startles the much smaller Korean across from Thorne. "Chill out dude, I will find out who's at the door."

The big gang leader rushes over to the door thinking, "Man this better be good!" He yanks it open in one swift agitated motion from not wanting the interruption.

"Cool it's you; I was just about to get pissed! Come on in Andy you're going to want to hear this!"

When they got to the dining room, Wayne gets up and shakes the Strife member's hand, "Hey what's up? It's been awhile dude!"

"Yeah man, I haven't seen you since we were peddling goods on the streets together!" Replies back Andy before taking a seat next to Thorne.

"Finish up Yoon on what you were saying so Collins can get the low down on what's happening!"

"As I was just saying Blue Hawk is the pig responsible for the killings of two of our men at Mark's pharmacy. An associate of mine told he was at Murphy's bar yesterday shooting pool with an old buddy from high school name Glenn Kinsky."

"What does this Kinsky have to do with anything?" Collins asked.

"According to what Glenn blabbed about at the local neighborhood tavern, he works on the South West side of town making leather jackets. Get this he works for a police officer's wife with the last name of Thomas!"

"Here's the deal Andy, not do we the Strangle Hold gang have issues with this Thomas cop but the Strife association have been busted by him also."

"So what are you scheming about in that evil mind of yours Thorne?"

"Let's get both of our gangs working together Collins in a joined team effort to pay back Blue Hawk! Together we can show a much greater display of organize brute force! He explains back in a loud psychotic manner!

"Fellas if we can pull this off it will be so bad ass!" Wayne says prior to letting out a quick laugh.

"Leave it to me Stuart I will let Bloodgood know of you would like to see come about between our two organizations. I'm fairly positive Jimmy isn't gunna have anything against knocking off Sergeant Thomas. He is still fuming about his younger brother who is sitting behind bars because of that pig!" Andy replies as he stands up from his chair preparing to leave the Strangle Hold leader's small dwelling.

"Just make sure he knows that I want to strike both the dirt bag man in blue and his old lady at the same night along with being close to the same time for the vicious assault!" Thorne speaks with excitement in his deep voice while he pounds on the table top using the palms of his large hands.

"I will arrange a meeting with Jimmy for next week to bring our gangs together to plot a well-executed assault. I'll catch you guys later then!" Andy turns and leaves without saying another word.

"Man this is so seriously crazy Thorne!" Yoon said preceding the two of them speaking further on the subject of killing Kevin.

The gang member gathering is set up the following week at a farm house out in the farmland North West of Portland on Sauvie Island at six pm on a Saturday.

It is Tony Barlotti's farm that has a huge red barn that serves as a methamphetamine lab. He allows the Strife gang to use the large building for their meeting because of the large quantities of meth that they sell for him.

At first he is reluctant about allowing the two gangs to use his property after catching wind of what their scheme is to embark on.

T-Boss as he's known in the drug world finally agrees but packs his meth lab from the huge red barn that is in back of the old two story Victorian house to a red Ford cargo van.

He leaves Tim Maxwell and Frank Carlyle to keep an eye on the place while he heads south to other illegal drug locations that he runs in Northern California.

Barlotti hopes that the vicious hit by the Portland gangs go well so it doesn't bring heat from the law into his money making illegal activity.

For all the times the middle men dope peddlers that are selling his illegal drugs were thrown in jail and his large quantity of meth or pot that have been confiscated because of law enforcement agents.

T-Boss wishes the gangs were going to murder all of Portland's narcotic officers in a swift strike. The narcs are making it hard for Tony's operation that deals cocaine, meth and marijuana to those who feel the need to use.

He'll be phoning back to his pair of loyal employees on Sauvie Island a week after the assault on Thomas to make sure everything is clear.

Being cautious is what has kept Barlotti from going back to the state penitentiary for selling large quantities of illegal drugs in the North West.

The day of the meeting at five fifty seven where Thorne and Bloodgood assemble a handful of the best criminals they have in their crime rings with guns.

It is taking place at the far south end of the old red barn deep within the spacious structure. There are two picnic tables that are put together side by side making on long table. On the dirty wall is a large paper map of the city of Portland pinned up for everyone to clearly view.

Strife's gang leader stands with his back to the map on the wall while Strangle Hold's head man sits at the end of the table close to where Bloodgood stands.

Tall skinny Jimmy brushes his long straight brown hair out of his eyes as he looks down at the rough looking audience that stares waiting for him to talk.

"Now that everybody is here I can begin plotting out this dirty deed scheme! This is going to be some dangerous shit that is going to go down dudes! Listen some of us may get hurt or killed in the process.

"That pig is going to die first before I do! I owe that bastard for putting me away for a fourteen month stretch!" A Mexican Strife member name Juan Martinez shouts out.

"I along with three other warriors am going to wait until Blue Hawk is all by his lonesome. He will have already dropped off his baby faced partner at the end of their shift. I wish my brother could be with me when I blow this cop's head off his shoulder!" Bloodgood declares.

"When do we get this party started brotha?" Jeff Ingram from the Strange Hold gang member inquires sitting next to his leader.

Thorne immediately stands from the picnic when witnesses Jimmy shrug not knowing the answer. The much smaller rival leader takes a seat letting the big man take charge of the gathering.

"Here's how I want it to go down fellas. Monday when he gets off work in the afternoon, his wife should be getting off around the same time. A dude I know has a couple of stolen rides that we can use across the river in Washington for a handful of change. Let's just say the cars are disposable like empty beer cans."

"Who will be doin what when this gets started dude?" One of the gang members asked from across the weathered picnic table.

Stuart uses his thick index finger to point out on the spread out city map, "This is where four armed Strife boys will be waiting in a vehicle three blocks from the North East police station. The ambush will take place on the route I've been informed Thomas always uses when he drives home."

"Me and my team of three other gents will be parked right here!" Thorne says pointing to a downtown South West location in Portland. "We will attempt to attack precisely the same time as the Strife team."

"Where exactly is the fuzze's girlfriend's house gunna be at Stuart?" Strangle Hold's Chris Nathanial asks with a puzzled look in his brown eyes.

"Dude you need wake up and get with program! We will be assaulting Blue Hawk's wife at her leather craft store dumb ass!"

Angrily he points to the city street that is a block east of Linn's business known as Eastern Delight Leathers at 1705 South West Broadway Street.

Their chosen sight will make it easy for him along with his three other gang members to get onto the freeway that is a straight shot exiting the city. The four of them will speed away north out of town if the plan goes well.

"Boss can I bring my Winchester pump twelve gauge on our little outing together?" Yoon asks.

"Not this time Wayne, we will be packing pistols that way we can easily conceal them walking to and from Mrs. Thomas's business." Thorne explains.

"Think there will be much cash at the leather shop?" Jeff Ingram asks.

"If there happens to be a large sum of money, then it's an added bonus that afternoon. Let me make myself very clear on this everyone!" Stuart says before he briefly pauses staring down at the criminals seated at the picnic tables before speaking again!

His expression shows how mean he can be while the protruding vein in his forehead displays an elevation in the large Strangle Hold leader's blood pressure.

It is a telltale sign of the Thorne's fervency on the subject at hand. "This is a mission of revenge on a so far lucky cop, boys! We are going to erase his lucky life in a couple of days showing a total vulgar display of violence!"

All of the gang bangers simultaneously get to their feet cheering with fists flaying in the air. They are loudly screaming out hateful things about Sergeant Thomas and his wife Linn.

CHAPTER 6 _____

The week that Kevin was off duty from being a police officer, just gives him an intermission to stew in the shootings that occurred at the pharmacy. He went to his local gym to work off his built-up frustration every day by exercising hard lifting free weights.

Thomas even spent a lot of time his wife at her shop, it was something he wanted to do for quite some time but couldn't because of his hectic schedule.

Wednesday December fourth Kevin is worried that he will possibly be fired from the 341st North Precinct for killing the two thugs at Mark's Pharmacy.

Hawk cannot shake the thought from his mind as he commutes in traffic to his police station in his black and white patrol car.

Before walking up to the Chief of Police's second floor office, Sergeant Thomas goes to the bathroom to adjust his uniform in front of the mirror.

Once in the office he is seated next to second in command Fred Nicklaus in front of the 162nd Division's man in charge's desk. Chief Duane Blythe is seated on the other side of the large metal desk with a serious look in his blue eyes.

It is five sixteen in the morning as Kevin nervously awaits his station's leader to begin to speak to him. "First of all, I believe you aware of why you have been requested for this formal get together with myself and Captain Nicklaus." Blythe states clearing the air.

"Yes, I am fully aware sir!" Hawk replies.

The Stocky overweight Chief picks up a beige paper folder up from the flat surface that's close to his bulging stomach that touches the edge. He nonchalantly flips it open then rummages through the paperwork inside to find what is after.

Blythe searches diligently until his fat fingers find the portion he is interested in making a point of to the uneasy feeling subordinate seated before him. "Oh yes, here it is Sergeant Thomas! According to your file here, it says you were an Airborne Ranger in the Vietnam War." He mentions upon glancing up from reading then briefly stares at Kevin awaiting his response.

"Yes chief that is correct sir."

"Your service records state that you were involved in a lot of intense firefights in combat situations over there." Kevin nods with a lump in his throat knowing what his superior is getting at.

"What I believe our chief is trying to say Sergeant is that we don't want any hero type of commandos recklessly killing the law breakers here in Portland." Captain Nicklaus chimes in to keep things rolling on what has to be said in the police station leader's fair size office.

"The citizens of our beloved city do not like reading about cops shooting people dead very often! Even if the individuals are armed career law breakers that use deadly force themselves!" Blythe adds.

"I fully understand what the two of you are saying to me this morning. I can assure you I do not want to play any kind of hero out on the streets! For me as a police officer, my personal goal each and every day is to bring those who break the law to justice using the judicial system." Thomas explains.

"How do you feel about the two individuals that lost their lives last Monday morning Sergeant?" The police Chief ask looking Kevin square in his eyes as he inquires his thoughts upon the use of deadly force.

"I truly wish I could have arrested each of the suspects without discharging my weapon in public that fateful morning causing bloodshed!" He explains to his superior officers showing sincerity as he has an earnest expression on his face while speaking to them!

"I am satisfied with the sentiment that the young Sergeant has displayed in front of me today Chief. One more thing, I really believe

Thomas did what he basically had to do to probably to keep himself from becoming a fatality!" Captain Nicklaus says.

"I firmly agree with your point of view Fred one hundred percent on his actions and I will type that in my report later today gentlemen! Do you have anything further to add on the subject Captain Nicklaus?"

"No I do not Chief! I have said everything I came in here to say on the subject sir!"

"Unless you have something more you feel you need to add Sergeant!" Blythe asked looking at Kevin.

"I have said what I need to say in this matter!"

"You are dismissed to go on duty with Deputy Davidson on your normal metro route!"

The overweight leader for the 162nd north east division stands up from the other side of his large metal desk extending his hand.

Hawk hurries to his feet giving the police chief and Captain Nicklaus each firm handshakes of appreciation. He thanks his superiors earnestly before exiting the office.

Trotting down the steps from the second floor, Thomas notices Davidson standing with his back facing him in the hallway at the bottom of the stairs.

"Looks like I still have a job here partner!" Kevin exclaims when he is near Gary at the first floor level. The veteran police Sergeant can't help but show his enthusiasm for being back on the force again.

"Darn it Thomas, I thought your ass was kicked out of here for sure!"

"They can't can me; I'm too well loved here!" After the statements the two shared a laugh together.

Sitting in the driver's seat of his number twelve squad car, felt pretty damn good to Hawk. Law enforcement work no matter how minuscule the crime he brings to justice provides him with a great sense of accomplishment.

"It is good to have you back boss!"

"I'm glad to be back again!"

While they are patrolling on north east Ratcliff Street they receive incoming call from dispatch saying, "We have a domestic dispute at 1947 Brookings drive."

"We are close by and are in route! We'll be at the scene in roughly five minutes time." Davidson says.

When they arrived at the residence, the pair of officers observes an intoxicated Hispanic man sitting on a badly stained light tan sofa.

He is belligerently speaking broken English while holding a can of domestic beer in his right hand. On the other side of the living room is a short chunky Mexican woman holding a blue wash cloth containing ice cubes to left cheek.

They first lead the crying lady to the kitchen for her statement away from her intimidating glaring spouse. "Miss, can you tell us what happen here today?" Davidson asks.

"My husband hit me twice in the face and verbally abused me in front of our children!" She tells them in strong Spanish accent as she wipes the tears from her brown eyes.

From the marks on her face, Kevin believes what she is telling them to be the absolute truth. Promptly the male subject is place under arrest as he vehemently denies laying a hand on his frightened wife.

The rest of the week for the most part is fairly easy going as far as being nonviolent. Patrol car twelve only dealt with misdemeanor citations such as speeding tickets among other moving violations.

Saturday December eleventh, Thomas took his wife to Mt. Hood for a weekend of downhill skiing with some friends and family for well needed getaway.

Monday evening just about five, Hawk is journeying east on Willamette Boulevard subsequent to dropping off Deputy Davidson at the police station's parking area.

He is heading home as usual to get ready for the Dragon's Fury Kung Fu studio. Master Charlie Lee will be testing Hawk and his wife for their black belt sashes, which the two have trained long and hard to reach the coveted mark.

Cruising by Wellesley Avenue motoring on Willamette St, Thomas notices through the pouring rain a large black 1966 four door Buick Delta 88 Sedan. It is two city blocks up head on the left parked next to the curb on Adams St.

The four door Sedan sticks out like sore thumb being parked next to a large run down vacant lot that is covered with gravel along with scattered garbage everywhere.

Thomas's intuition gives him the notion that something seems a bit peculiar about the way the Delta 88 quickly pulls out from the dirty curb.

He observes the Buick waiting at the graffiti covered red stop sign that leads to the street he steadily travels upon. Hawk passes the car full of rough looking characters with an uneasy feeling in his gut.

Thomas looked the car full of thugs over as best he could in the short of amount of time that he had in motion. Seconds later the Portland Police Sergeant gazes into his rear view mirror, observing the black vehicle rapidly make a left turn onto his path of travel.

In no time at all the large Delta 88 gains a vast amount of ground behind his black and white cruiser. Kevin instinctively unlatches the bracket that securely holds the pump action twelve gauge shot gun that is loaded with six slug rounds.

The weapon remains stable in its mount that is bolted to the vehicle's floor board in the middle section standing upright at a forty five degree angle.

A quick tug upward could easily remove the powerful weapon of destruction now if he requires the use of it once he has to rapidly exit from the vehicle.

Suddenly the sound of rapid fire sharply is heard coming from the rear striking the trunk of Thomas's patrol car. He hurries; sinking down as low as he possibly can while still viewing the road ahead of him.

Hawk stomps his foot down hard on the Chevrolet's black rubber gas pedal to gain more distance from the men who are trying to end his life.

Numerous rounds crash through the rear window of the police cruiser from the would be assassins. They are shooting at will from only two car lengths behind the one they refer to as "Blue Hawk".

Juan Martinez a low man for the Strife gang is the driver of the stolen four door Sedan. He is the only street punk that isn't shooting a gun out of a rolled down window as the Buick speeds along.

Martinez is busy looking through the windshield as the pair of wipers work fast to clear the pouring rain off as he attempts to catch up to the hated police Sergeant.

Kevin senses the stinging sensation of a hot nine millimeter full metal jacket slug penetrate the right tricep of his tone muscular arm. A split second later a large caliber bullet tears a deep gash through Thomas's flesh when it wings the left side of his head.

The warm thick blood oozes from both of Hawk's painful wounds while he maneuvers the issued car to avoid the shooter's deadly barrage of rounds.

"Nooo, I'm not going out this way!" He yells out at the top of his lungs displaying fervent anger in his dilemma.

Kevin manages to floor it putting more distances between him and his would be assassins that are giving it all they have firing rapidly at him.

Simultaneously cranking on the steering wheel to the right then stomping down hard on the squad car's brake pedal, an evasive maneuver he learned at his police academy.

The black and white Caprice travels fast in a one eighty degree skid on the thin layer of water that coats the black asphalt of the North West city's street.

It feels as if he is moving in slow motion as the vehicle slams the left rear wheel extremely hard against the concrete curb. Instantly a loud pop sound comes from the tire as it is punctured from the powerful impact.

In the blink of an eye, Hawk is out of the number twelve squad car shooting the twelve gauge pump. Juan steps on the accelerator when he notices "Blue Hawk" jump out with shot gun moving to the rear of the patrol car.

Hard rain continuously comes down as the wounded patrol man leans over the black trunk aiming and shooting at the moving Buick.

Andy Collins is leaning his stocky body out the open window of the rear passenger side doing his best to land a deadly shot to finish Kevin off.

An accurately placed slug hits Andy directly center of his broad forehead that travels through blowing out a very large hole out the back of his cranium. Blood and brains fly through the cold wet air making a mess on the stolen car.

Thomas's fourth and final shot shatters the rear window fatally striking the Black Mamba gang banger that's riding in the back seat.

He is hit in the side of the head by the large caliber round sending him flying forward into Martinez as he drives the Delta as fast as he can while fleeing the scene.

Hawk is forced to quit shooting when the bad guys are well out of range of his low velocity weapon. Dizziness sets in as he staggers himself back to the car driver's seat.

Using a shaky hand Kevin manages to pick up the CB radio's mic, "This is Sergeant Thomas of car number twelve; I have been shot twice by men who are now fleeing in a black 1966 four door Buick Delta 88 over!" He says speaking slow as he slurs his words from the head injury as well as a loss of blood.

"Lieutenant Gronich here, what is your present location Sergeant Thomas?"

Looking around trying to focus his blurry eyes on the street signs nearby him before pushing the button on the CB radio mic, "I'm on Willamette St between Allen and Mosley."

"I'll be there shortly Sergeant, hold tight for a few over! I'm going to radio out for an ambulance for you!"

"Roger that Lieutenant over and out!"

Kevin grabbed a navy blue bandana from his back pocket, pressed it tight against the gash in the side of his bicep that was created by the bullet.

His dizziness along has intensified along with felling very faint from the loss of blood from the wounds he has sustained from the street wise punks.

Deciding to try to sit down from his kneeling position on the passenger side of his cruiser Kevin slowly moves to the sitting position as his sight goes black.

Voices enter his ears prior to Hawk slowly opening his eyes as he is in route to the hospital in the back of a fast moving ambulance. Thomas's unfocused blue eyes only briefing see the female and male EMT techs previous to passing out again for several more hours.

CHAPTER 7 _____

Two days after the attack Kevin wakes up on the firm single wide hospital bed at St. Marcos community medical center on the south east side of Portland. He is wearing a thin cotton hospital gown; there is a long transparent rubber tube stuck in his right arm that leads to a quarter full IV bag.

Thomas turns his head gazing to the right side of the small sterile room. Standing beside his bed is Detective Chad Armstrong, who is looking down at the injured police officer expressing a sullen look.

He is holding a flip open spiral notepad in his left hand and a black ink pen in his right close to chest high. "So how are you feeling?"

"Like I've been hit by a Tri-Met bus full of overweight passengers."

"In no time at all you will be feeling much better; anyway I need to ask you a few questions. Do you have any idea why the Strife gang would target you?"

"The only thing I can think of is the numerous arrests on their members for various crimes. I take it you have leads that the gang were the shooters."

"We found the Buick that was used as the vehicle parked three miles from the scene with Andy Collins, part of his head missing from your shot. He was lifeless when found at the site on NE 57th St. Tyrese Jackson was sitting next to Collins clinging on to life from his injury. He died before arriving at the hospital that day."

"I had seen two people in the front seat of the Delta 88 in my rear view mirror when it came up behind me that I couldn't clearly make out. Though I'm pretty sure it was Jimmy Bloodgood riding shotgun in the chasing vehicle."

"Has anybody contacted my wife to let her know where I'm at right now Detective?"

"I can't begin to express how very sorry I am about what happened to Linn!"

Thomas's stomach drops and he has a sore lump in his throat, "What the hell do you mean Armstrong?" The concerned Police Sergeant subsequently sits up in bed feeling much more alert to hear Chad's reply.

"There was an armed robbery at your wife's leather craft business right around the same time you were being ambushed."

"Is my wife ok?"

"This isn't easy for me to tell you Sergeant Thomas! She was shot and killed along with a female employee by the name of Marie Garcia. The lone survivor of the robbery is Glenn Kinsky who was shot next to his sewing machine!"

"How many men were there?" Hawk inquires as tears drip from his angry eyes.

"As of now we don't have a precise number on how many subjects were involved, only that there were two different calibers of weapons used. So far we don't have enough evidence to link anyone to the crime yet Sergeant. Again I'm sorry for your loss!"

"Thank you very much Detective Armstrong!" Kevin tells him prior to the medium built man turning and making his way out the hospital room.

A weak Police Sergeant is alone with his thoughts for a little less than an hour with a range of emotions coming over him from the loss of his loving wife.

As Kevin is thinking about what kind of approach he is going to use to seek out vindication when a sandy blonde haired heavy nurse walks in.

She is dressed in a white hospital dress that has a black plastic name tag with white lettering that reads Nancy Evans, "How are you doing this morning Mr. Thomas?"

"My body aches all over and I can hardly move without the room starting to spin around."

"You did have a nasty head injury along with a great deal of blood loss when you were brought in here. It won't be but a week or so before you will be up and moving about."

"One way or another I'll be on my feet sooner than that time frame Nurse Evans! I've got some very important things that I need to take care of in the worst kind of way!"

When Nancy was finished routinely checking on Hawks vital signs, Davidson ambulated through the door to see how his superior is doing.

He sees his tall partner lying down in a weakened state covered up with blankets with things attached to him. "Man, you'll do anything to get out of work, won't you?"

"Rookie you're a wise ass even at the worst times in my pathetic life!"

"Sorry Sergeant Thomas! This kind of scene really isn't easy for me to deal with!"

"Don't sweat it Gary, I could use a little cheering up right now anyway."

"I just came from Glenn Kinsky room?"

"How's the guy doing partner?"

"His head is wrapped up like yours. Kinsky got out of surgery a little bit ago and is in a deep sleep from the anesthetic."

"What room do they have him in Davidson?"

"He is currently upstairs in room 401 sharing the occupancy with an elderly man who is in a catatonic state in the intensive care unit. Glenn's doctor informed me he doesn't anticipate him gaining consciousness for many hours and doesn't want him disturbed until tomorrow."

"Kinsky is one person I definitely need speak with to find out if he viewed any of the scum bags faces!"

Deputy Davidson visits Sergeant Thomas for a little more than an half an hour before getting back on patrol with another police officer.

An older looking doctor strolls into Kevin's patient room carrying a brown folder at his side. He is a clean shaven medium built man with short salt and pepper hair wearing a long white lab coat that is open.

A petite older looking nurse is walking close behind the well groomed physician carrying a red plastic tray. It has a white ceramic plate with scrambled eggs, toast and bacon on it. Next to the breakfast is a small glass of orange juice.

"Good Morning Mr. Thomas, my name is Dr. Allen Wright! You are looking much better than you appeared the other day I seen you!"

"I could probably use a shave doc!" Hawk rubs his right hand over his stubbly cheek that he usually shaves every morning whether he works or not. Wright chuckles a little at the comment he made.

The nurse sets the tray down in front of the police officer to eat while the physician is talking to Thomas. She briskly leaves after placing a flexible plastic straw into the orange juice for him to sip from.

"When I woke up I was feeling pretty damn woozy and had trouble getting my eyes to focus for a little while. Now that I've been up for a bit things are becoming much more normal for me."

"That's very common for someone to experience when they have sustained a bad head injury, such as a bullet bouncing off the skull with great force."

"So when can I be discharged from here doctor?"

"I looked over your medical charts prior to coming in here Kevin and my opinion is that you are well enough to go home this afternoon.

After the doctor leaves Thomas realizes the only clothes he has at the hospital is the bloody uniform he was brought in wearing two days ago.

Kevin calls up the Credit Union where his father is the manager. It is only four miles from his house on the same side of Portland he used to share with Linn.

"Hello, may I help you?"

"May I speak with William Thomas please?"

"Can I ask whose calling sir?"

"I am his youngest son!"

"Just one moment!"

A few seconds later, Hawk hears his dad speaking on the other side of the phone, "Hey Kev, what's going on? This is an odd time of the day for you to give me a ring! Is everything ok?"

"As a matter of fact I'm at the St. Marcos hospital!"

"What in the world happened son?"

"Oh, I was shot in a couple of places. It's not the first time for me dad."

"Does Linn know where you are at right now?"

A sickening feeling sets in to the pit of Kevin's stomach as well as his eyes water up preceding answering the unwanted question. "I'm sorry to tell you, she was killed at her shop along with another employee when her business was robbed at gun point."

"Who in their right minds would do such an awful thing to such sweet young lady?"

"Father the lowest kind of trash in the city! When I find out who's responsible for her murder, everyone involved will pay dearly for it!"

"Is there anything I can do for you son?"

Thomas takes a calming deep breath subsequent to saying another word, "As a matter of fact what I need you to do for me is when you can make the time, pick up a change of casual clothes for me at my house."

"Son I don't have a key to your house."

"There is a spare for the front door under the brown mat that is lying on the back patio just in front of the sliding glass door."

"What kind of clothing do you want me to bring to you?"

"Casual street clothes, a pair of blue jeans, tee shirt tube socks, denim jacket and my black hi top basketball shoes. All the clothes are easy to find in my bedroom."

"Shouldn't be a problem to do son, I will take an early lunch to make the clothing run for you."

"Thank you very much for doing this for me dad!"

"Not a problem at all! I'm on way buddy!" William tells him then swiftly hangs up the receiver.

Thirty minutes later, Sergeant Thomas's dad is strolling into his hospital room with a dark blue duffle bag at his side. The bag's black handles are gripped in his left hand with the clothing zipped up inside.

Kevin at that time still has his IV inserted from the vein of his right arm as well as the electrocardiograph's sensor pads taped to his hairy muscular chest monitoring his heart.

William's son reaches up his heavy feeling arm grabbing the handle's the gym bag, "Thanks dad! Without you I would probably have to walk out of here looking like a slaughter house worker."

A short time after Mr. Thomas's arrival, a nurse shows professional courtesy removing the medical devices off the eager patient's body.

Hawk gets up from his inclined bed, putting his bare feet onto the cold shiny tile floor. His knees feel a little shaky as he stands stationary for a moment while he gets his bearing back to begin moving.

"Please excuse me for a moment pop, I'll just go slap these on so we can get the heck out of here." Kevin says before mildly staggering to the tiny restroom to change into his street clothes.

Thomas goes into the bathroom, shuts the door then rushes to get out of the thin revealing hospital gown that makes him feel a bit feminine.

"Now this is more like it!" Kevin exclaims patting the front of the grey tee shirt with the palms of his hands in succession to exiting the small rest room wearing his own threads.

"Feel like a new man don't you son putting on a fresh change of clothing."

"Man you got that right! I felt pretty darn funny wearing that woman's night gown!" Hawk explains exhibiting a slight smile across his lips.

After filling out the forms, William takes his son home briefly staying to comfort him in his time of need. "Give me a call later and we will work out funeral arrangements."

"I would appreciate the help dad, please break the news to mom gently! Linn's death is going to crush her greatly when she hears about it!"

"I'll tell her as graciously as I can! I have to get back to the office now I have a ton of paper work to get done!"

That afternoon depression hit the police sergeant hard as he sat on his wife's side of the bed looking at a picture of the two of them together in Saigon.

Loneliness with the sad sense of loss brought Kevin to heavy sobbing as his outlook for his future is dark without his beautiful wife to be there.

CHAPTER 8 _____

The next day Hawk drove to St. Marcus hospital at nine in the morning still wearing the clothing his father brought him the day before. Kevin parks his fast 65' Chevy Impala next to an orange Datsun hatchback in the middle portion of the parking lot.

He swiftly enters the medical center's sliding automatic glass doors having the appearance of a wounded patient. His motive for being there is to speak with Glenn Kinsky, to find out what he remembers about the shooting that unfortunate afternoon.

Inside the hospital's spacious lobby, the tall muscular man briskly ambulates to the elevator carrying a black flip open notepad and pen tightly in his right hand.

His mind nonstop wonders what Kinsky god willing might have retained from the crime that was committed. Using a rigid index finger the Portland police officer gives the up button a hard poke for the elevator to come down.

While anxiously waiting, a man and his young son stroll up standing next to Thomas. The little boy is carrying a basket full of bright yellow flowers telling his father how much he thinks his mommy will love them.

When the stainless steel doors open Hawk allows the pair to go ahead of him into the compartment, he strolls in then presses the fourth floor button.

In the hallway of the intensive care ward he walks by many wide wooden patient doors that are shut. 401 is at the end of the broad hallway he realizes he looks at the posted room numbers on the wall.

Turning the oval shaped brass handle, Hawk gently pushes the wide heavy tan door casually walking in. Upon entering he sees an average height Caucasian doctor that's wearing a light blue hospital scrubs.

The thirty something physician is preoccupied opening each of Glenn's closed eye lids checking his pupils for dilation. He is shining a small black metal flash light into the scruffy bearded young man's brown eyes.

After looking over the long haired patient, the doctor turns around noticing Kevin standing across the room in the doorway, "Hi, my name is Dr. Steven Vanmire. Are you a friend or relative of Mr. Kinsky?" Vanmire inquires as he adjusts his wire frame glasses.

"Actually I am neither; I'm Sergeant Thomas from the Portland third precinct." He flips open his worn leather bill fold that has his shiny gold badge that it is pinned to the inner wall.

Kevin holds it up between his thumb and forefinger for the medical professional to view as he perambulated closer to the off duty police officer.

Vanmire runs his eyes over the badge that is being held for him to examine quickly determining that it is authentic, "Is there anything that I may help you with officer?"

"What I really need to do is ask Glenn a few questions this morning!"

"Be my guest but he is in serious condition right now."

"I'm actually surprised he's still alive doc!"

"I don't know how long he will stay that way Sergeant Thomas the victim is not out of the woods yet!"

"Looking at the shaved spots where the incisions were made tells me you guys had to dig around in that skull of his. He is one tough dude for lasting this long from taking a large caliber bullet to the brain!"

"I assisted Chief Surgeon Hansen yesterday for nearly three hours of surgery removing the nine millimeter bullet. There was also the abstraction of shattered bone fragments within the inner wall of his cranium. We put two pieces of surgical tubing into his skull to relive the pressure off of his swollen brain. I'll tell you to the right portion of Mr. Kinsky's head did a tremendous amount of irreversible damage."

Kevin casually strolls up close to Kinsky's bedside with the notepad resting in the palm of his hand. He scoots a cushioned arm chair next to the hospital bed ensuing slowly sits down making his aching body comfortable.

Looking at the resting patient he begins talking to him nonchalantly trying to get a response from the badly injured man lying on his back.

Almost thirty minutes lapse by when Glenn slowly opens his eyes gazing over to where the sound is coming from beside him.

His brown blood shot eyes have a drowsy lost look in them while he blankly stares at Hawk. Kinsky has the appearance of a person that has had way too much alcohol to drink.

"Hi, its Kevin Thomas remember me?"

"You are Linn's husband right!" He says with a hoarse faint voice that is barely audible.

"Glenn did you see any of their faces the night the low life's mercilessly shot everyone at Eastern Delight Leathers?"

Glenn closes his eyes for a few seconds trying to remember the tragic event. He opens his eyes looking back to Hawk who is on pins and needles waiting to hear what he has to say to him.

"All four men were wearing ski masks and moving around quickly man!" Kinsky says then coughs a couple of times hard dislodging blood and mucus from his lungs.

"I know this is difficult for you! Please try to recall anything distinctive about the armed men!"

Slowly the wounded hippie turns his head looking straight up at the white ceiling above his bed. A long silent pause occurs causing Hawk to stand up from the chair from the anticipation that's getting on his nerves.

"Dude, it happened all so fast that day! Right now my brain spinning circles in my head as I try to think!"

"Are you or have you ever affiliated with any kind organize gang? Please tell me if have any idea who would want to bring harm to a small business that you worked in!"

"No, but I know fellas I went to school with that are tied in with local gangs. Oh yeah! I was at Murphy's bar playing pool with Leo

Stanton telling him I work for a cop's wife with the last name of Thomas."

"What do you know about this Stanton?"

"My older brother Josh used to sell dope on the streets for a Korean gang banger that has a black belt in Tae Kwon Do."

"Does Wayne Yoon ring a bell?"

The EKG meter starts beeping indicating that Glenn's heart rate has slowed down quite a bit as he begins passing out. "Kinsky! Kinsky! Tell me if Yoon was involved in killing my wife!" Hawk shouts out as he shakes Linn's injured employee's right shoulder to keep him conscious.

"Contact my brother!" Glenn softly says in a gravelly voice that's hard to understand.

The machine Kinsky's hooked to is displaying a thin flat line when Doctor Vanmire rushes in with an assisting nurse whose wheeling in a defibrillator. Kevin helplessly stands out of the way while the doctor futilely makes an attempt to resuscitate the dying patient.

Minutes later the Police Sergeant leaves the small room when it is apparent the thin long haired guy would never take another breath on this earth.

Walking across the rain soaked asphalt of the hospital parking area to his two door Sedan carrying his notes. He would glance once or twice at the name Josh Kinsky that he wrote down in black ink.

"Josh Kinsky, I bet you're the drug peddler that I helped book a few years ago that Lieutenant Gronich brought into our 162nd Station."

Upon tossing down the notepad on the dark vinyl bucket seat beside him in his souped up Chevy. Roaring out the parking lot, Hawk has a crazed look in his eyes to go with the three days of stubble on his face.

He steps a little hard on the gas pedal slightly spinning the rear tires to get into traffic making his way to the North East police precinct.

At the station, Thomas wastes no time hurrying into Detective Chad Armstrong's office he shares with three other investigators on the first floor.

"Sergeant you're a sight for sore eyes! You look like a man that just came out of the jungle!"

"Been there done that buddy! Not this time, though I feel that way my friend!" Kevin strolls over to the full pot of coffee on the dirty stained counter top at the right corner of the cluttered room.

He pours himself a hot black cup of coffee into a random well used ceramic cup, takes a sip then strolls to where Armstrong is seated, "This stuff as strong as gasoline but after tossing and turning last night I need something to keep me awake."

"Shit I use that stuff to survive this job full of long tedious hours!"

"What have you turned up since the last time I talked to you at the hospital?"

"We know that both the Strangle Hold and the Strife gang were involved in the massacre at Linn's business as well as the attempt on your life."

"How in the hell do you know about that?"

"You're gunna like this one! Staff Sergeant Wilson spotted Lisa Philmore turning tricks on South East 142nd St. After being searched by a female officer a large size rock of crack cocaine is found in her bra. Our beloved Staff Sergeant gives the skinny street walker the riot act about what she will be charged with before placing her in the back seat."

"So who in god's name is this Lisa character?"

"She is one Stuart Thorne's new girls that came down from Seattle. Here at the station I personally had the scared looking hooker placed into a quiet little interrogation room with yours truly."

"Did you give her the stone face look as you made her feel like a sinking ship in the sea of justice?"

"Sounds like you know my routine buddy! Anyhow I explained that I knew she was selling her body for Thorne. At first she played dumb until I explained that I would be able to drop charges if she could answer my questions."

"Please tell me you had her singing like a bird!"

"Lisa told me she was lying in Stuart's bedroom after they had sex when she overheard Stuart making plans with Yoon in the dining room. I asked if something mentioned about a leather shop, she responded by saying yes!"

"Those rotten sons of bitches! I had a gut feeling they were behind this all along!" Thomas clinched his fists in anger as his face turned red standing next to the department's head detective.

"When I inquired if she heard about a shooting plot against a Portland Police officer by the name of Kevin Thomas, Philmore replied "I have never heard that name in my life. The dude by the name of Blue Hawk is what I overheard. Stuart shouted out the name in his dining room saying the man was going to bleed all over the city's street.

"Did she know at that time where Thorne was shacking up at with his murdering buddies?"

"Lisa only caught wind that the gang leader is somewhere out of town in a rural location north of Portland. Sounds like the punks are hiding out until it cools off for them."

"The only thing that's going to cool off is the dirt bags that killed Linn in cold blood!"

"I know how upset you must be from loss of your wife but this case it has to be handled by the book. Please remember that you are first an officer of the law! Don't do something dumb that will affect your career!"

Gary suddenly pops into the room wearing casual clothes appearing to be in his usual happy go lucky mood displaying a goofy grin on his thin lips. "I hope you gents aren't talking about me again!"

"Why would we talk behind your back rookie when it's much more fun to do it to your face!"

All three men are chuckling as the presence of the young deputy lightens the serious mood up. "Thank you for the info Detective. I'll catch you later!"

"You got it Thomas!"

Hawk and his partner stride out into the hallway leaving Armstrong's to his paperwork at his desk. "Hey where ya headed Sarg?" Gary asks as he's being lead in the direction of the large administration office.

"I need to go to the records room to look up a person of interest that may help clear things up for me!"

"Cool, I got to go that way anyway to pick up my pay check from the bookkeeper."

"Why aren't you working the beat right now?"

"Because of you my schedule is a total wreck; I ride with whoever is available to partner up with on patrol."

In the administration office, Davidson goes to the payroll accountant's desk while Kevin walks to the other side of the room. Hawk begins looking over the front of the tall sheet metal filing cabinets seeking the drawer with the last name begin with the letter K on it.

Following pulling out a couple of drawers, he finds the off color white folder containing Josh Kinsky's records. Wasting no time Thomas pulls out Glenn's older brothers file flopping it onto an unused office desk.

Sitting down on an old hard wooden roll around chair the Police Sergeant scoots forward close to the desk then rummages through the paperwork inside.

Upon finding what may be useful, he writes down Josh's address and phone number in his pocket size notepad. The information is from when the illegal drug peddler was arrested two years previously.

"Hopefully I can use this to get of hold of this knucklehead! If not there are other methods to use in finding him in a large city like this." He thinks to himself while putting the folder back into its rightful place.

"Find what you're looking for boss?" Gary says strolling up behind Kevin as shuts the long drawer.

"Might be something here in my hand to help me with my search but I'm still going to roam the neighborhoods seeking justice for what happened!"

"If you don't mind the company I would like to ride shotgun spotting bad guys for you."

"For me I'm happy to have you come along on my off duty quest, though you might get yourself in trouble along with myself."

"I can't help but want to aid you in finding the bastards that committed the horrific crime against you and Linn."

"Come along then let's do some cruising in my Chevy to see what we can turn up buddy."

The pair nonchalantly strolls to the back side of the parking lot to the awaiting metallic red Impala that is parked next to a couple of broke down police cruisers.

CHAPTER 9 _____

Hawk slowly drives out of the lot with the radio turned off as he they nervously around to see if anyone is watching. "I hope I don't get shot as you chauffeur me around." Davidson replies three blocks from their northeast 162nd police station.

"Tell you what, when the bullets start flying I'll jump out of the vehicle with my target sign tee-shirt on waving it's me that you're after."

Gary begins shaking his head at the humorous absurd thing that was just said. "Wow! I thought I was a big smart ass!"

"Kid you rubbed off on me since we've been working together playing the good guys."

"All joking aside, what if we do take gun fire?"

"My trustee .45 is on my side here and if it becomes a fierce fire fight my friend you have my permission to utilized my back up .38 revolver in the glove compartment."

It is a dark cloudy overcast day as they travel by a small grungy convenient store that has steel bars over the windows with beer advertisement all over the building.

The pair of off duty cops are scanning back and forth from one side of the street to the other passing by small older one story homes.

Davidson notices a pedestrian that is shuffling toward the two of them he moves with true gangster style as he strides on the concrete surface. Up ahead is a short petite built young man dressed in a pricey casual grey suit wearing shiny black dress shoes on his small feet. The

Stylish Korean sticks out like a sore thumb with the attire he has on when everybody else wears jeans and tee-shirts.

"That son of bitch looks familiar to me right there!" Davidson speaks up saying while he points in the direction of the pedestrian.

Kevin presses lightly on the brake pedal slightly slowing the two door sedan when he realizes its Wayne Yoon walking down the street. The lone drug dealer pays no attention to the two plain clothes police men driving by in the dark red hot rod.

Hawk pulls into an empty driveway, backs out to motor up behind the unaware Strangle Hold member. Thomas parks his Impala next to the curb fifty yards in front of Yoon who is strolling along displaying an expression on his face of having a bad attitude.

"Wait in the car Deputy this won't take long!"

"Not a problem Sergeant!"

Hawk's adrenaline is flowing as he hops out of the driver's door of his car knowing there is a possibility of the encounter becoming physical. Briskly he perambulates around the back side of the Chevrolet making his way to the sidewalk.

The tall stocky police officer stops the much smaller street hood to pressure the Korean gang banger for answers. "What the hell do you want from me "Blue Hawk"? Shouldn't you be wearing your dark blue uniform?"

"I have a few questions for you?"

"I say nothin to you! I know nothin what so ever Mr. police officer man!" Yoon declares in a condescending tone looking up at Sergeant Thomas smugly.

Suddenly Wayne quickly tries to side step past Kevin showing a total disregard for the police sergeant.

"Hey just a minute, I'm not done speaking with you yet!" He says placing his left hand on the drug dealer's chest gently to have Yoon stop walking.

In a rapid fluid motion the wiry drug dealer knocks away the off duty police officer's large hand followed by a hard closed fist back hand to the side of Hawk's mouth.

Yoon is standing in a martial art ready stance on the sidewalk less than three feet before him appearing to be set for a street fight.

"So this is how you want it to go down today!" Kevin says surprisingly calm while feeling the sting of the blow while standing in a Kung Fu fighting stance.

"Come at me I kick your ass good for you pig!"

Kevin showing that a big man can move fast swiftly performed a powerful side kick hitting the gang member hard in the stomach.

The pair boxed back and forth each throwing kicks combined with quick punches both demonstrating great martial art technique. They both seem to be almost landing shot for shot on the narrow concrete sidewalk.

Wayne lands a hard spinning jump kick that squarely connects to Kevin's gunshot wound causing the sewn up gash to weep out blood.

He began seeing stars from the powerful impact of the black leather dress shoes smashing against the left side of his close clipped head.

The kicked pissed Thomas off motivating him to move in faster with shots as well as striking harder at the smaller opponent.

Hawk fakes as if he was going to step to perform a side kick but instead does a powerful spinning back hand. Yoon moves to block the seemingly predictable movement never noticing the fist that lands hard against the side of his right eye staggering the street punk.

Thomas finishes the drug dealer off by performing a fast spinning round house kick that strikes him on the right side of the mouth. Wayne flies backward landing on his back flat on the cold damp concrete close to being knocked out.

Rushing to the fallen drug dealer Hawk rolls him onto his thin belly.

He wastes no time putting the Strangle Hold members left arm behind his back, starts placing hard downward pressure on Yoon's elbow joint. "AAAHHH, you're going to break my arm!" He says hollering out in agony.

"Where are your buddies, the ones that shot me and senselessly murdered my wife!"

"AAAHH, AAAHH! I don't know anything!"

"I don't believe what you are spitting out of your lying lips!" Kevin loudly states then uses his strong left hand to apply pressure to the back of Yoon's left hand while still having his elbow joint firmly locked in place.

The pain for the Korean American street hustler becomes a lot more intense for him to deal with when the police Sergeant's knee in his back. Hawk knows all too well how to use joint manipulation to create intense pain on a subject from hours of practice.

"Alright, I tell you what you want. Please stop bending down on my wrists Blue Hawk!" Thomas eases up on pressure so Wayne can relay some information to him without screaming out in pain as he tries to speak.

"They are at some farm on Sauvie Island!"

"Give me the damn address or I'll snap your arm like a twig punk!" He adds more force once again to Yoon's two joints. "AAAHHH, I can't remember the exact address! I've only been there a couple of times, both times I was stoned! I swear to you!"

"You better not be lying to me! If I find out that you are hiding something from me, the next time we meet won't be nearly as pleasant!"

Thomas hears a short distance away the metallic sound of his Chevrolet's passenger door opening. "Whatever you're doing you better get a move on before we have a full scale riot on our hands!" Deputy Davidson says in succession to perambulating closer to the superior officer.

Kevin glances to the right after helping Wayne to his feet then notices a small crowd of rough looking young men in their early twenties. They are staring in his direction from the corner of the street a block away on the opposite side of the road.

Some are holding quart bottle of beers that are covered by small brown paper bags to conceal the contents of what they are drinking.

When the police sergeant is almost to the parked two door Sedan, Wayne starts yelling out things like, "You can kiss my ass filthy pig bastard!" The short Strangle Hold member screams out with several other obscenities while flipping him off the man that got the better of him.

Hawk only briefly gazes back at the verbal dealer with the bloody mouth that drips down onto the black hairs of his thin goatee.

Calm and nonchalantly the tall man, who is on a mission, strolls away ignoring Yoon who is standing rigid demonstrating his dislike for the police officer.

He could care less about Wayne right now, his mind is fully focused on the all the gang bangers that they think their safe being out of the city.

Thomas follows his partner's lead by getting into the Impala closing the door upon sitting once again behind the steering wheel of the mean street machine.

"Did the dirt bag give out any useful information after the altercation Sergeant?" Gary inquires as the red Chevy pulls away from the busted up concrete curb.

"As a matter fact the tough little thug spit out something I can use after I gave him an incentive to talk. Back there you showed a little fear Rookie about the group on the street corner down from us."

"Sorry boss I was just trying to prevent any hostile aggression against us by an angry mob."

"Next time deputy, please try to give off the appearance of someone fully in control as well as not worried about your surroundings. It's ok to be scared in a situation but criminals feed off that fear out on the street!"

"You have made your point clear to me Sergeant Thomas.

I will work on exhibiting a tougher outward appearance around aggressive people."

Conversions between the two men are lighter for the rest of ride to the police station parking area. A black and white cruiser is slowly cruising out the exit as Kevin pulls in to a spot next to his partner's private vehicle.

"If you need my help for catching these perpetrators off duty I'll do whatever I can to assist in the matter! As for me, I really don't care if it costs me my job! What was done to you Sergeant turns my stomach!"

"Thank you so much for that offer partner, but I'm just gathering information to give to our department's detectives before I leave." Sergeant Thomas explains to his partner not wanting to involve the younger officer in his real bloody vendetta that's to go down.

"Where are you headed to?"

"I've made arrangements to take Linn's things back to her home country of South Vietnam. I wish to personally pay my respect to my wife's family about this unfortunate event."

"How much time did you request off?"

"One full week following the end of my suspension which still has six days left, Captain Nicklaus told me that it looks good for me coming back with a clear record."

"Once again I'm very sorry about your wife, if there is anything that I can do for you don't hesitate to call!"

"Thank you Davidson, I might just do that! I'll see you when I get back!"

"Have a safe trip all the way over there, I will catch you when your back here in your sharp looking uniform." The deputy says prior to shaking his superior's hand. Gary exits the Impala strolling to his car not looking back as Hawk backs out from the spot to leave.

CHAPTER 10

On the way home Kevin mulls over in his mind that he needs to call, how he is going to ask his buddy for help to able him in his pay back plot along with plans that deal with Linn's funeral service.

Slowly Hawk cruises onto his single car concrete driveway shutting off the Chevy's V8 engine. He sits still staring at his home's white painted front door when a memory from a few years popped into his head.

Thomas begins remembering one of the times he came home from a riot control assignment that erupted into violence in downtown Portland.

As soon as his car began turning into their driveway a crazed petite Linn is running to greet her husband who is still wearing his riot gear.

Telling him how worried she was from watching the news coverage on TV that showed the protestors fighting the police men as she cried. It touched Kevin deeply that his young wife cared so much for him to react the way she did.

At the front door Hawk stands with the front door key in his shaky right hand not looking forward to going into the house he once shared with the love of his life.

Entering the dark living room he hurries straight to the phone on the counter by the kitchen, turns on the brown lamp with a white shade.

He notices that the red digital display reads seven new messages on the answering machine. Ignoring it the Police Sergeant dials up his father first. "Hello dad!"

"Hey what's up son?"

"There is a change of plans; I just want Linn's body to be cremated so her remains can be sent to her mother's village that's close to Saigon."

""Shouldn't be a problem what so ever. When you get to Vietnam tell Linn's family how sorry your mother and I are of her passing."

"I'll certainly make sure that I do that dad. Thanks again for all of your help."

"You're very welcome buddy. Anything that I can do to help you just give me a ring!"

"Thanks, I will talk to you later."

"Good by Kev."

After talking to his dad, Kevin calls up the Portland airport setting up a round trip to Ho Chi Minh City. The rough overcrowded city is where he first met Linn falling head over heels in love with the pretty teenage girl.

For close to an hour of speaking with a soft speaking sales representative for an airline who is trying to find him the best rate for a sudden departure. An understanding Hawk buys a high price round trip ticket for what the airlines refer to as a commuter sudden departure.

Thomas's flight will leave from Portland Thursday morning at four-thirty on Air World Airline Flight #74 at gate number 24. He scribbles down the information on a piece of paper as well as the confirmation number after giving her his credit card number.

Subsequent to hanging up the receiver, the anguished man dials up his martial arts instructor telling him the bad news about his wife. He tells instructor Lee of his coming trip out of the country and wishes to make further plans when he arrives back in the United States.

Charlie tells his grieving student that the Dragon's Fury studio will be here when he feels mentally ready to train in self-defense.

Upon taking a long hot shower that afternoon to unwind a bit, the Police Sergeant takes his .45 automatic apart thoroughly cleaning it every piece to the pistol.

Kevin knows he can't take his service handgun to kill the gang members all with it. Following resembling the weapon Hawk puts it in its holster then slides the stainless steel Colt under his queen size bed.

"I have two more calls that I need to make, I sure in the hell can't make them here! They will have to be made at the telephone booth on the corner six blocks from my house. I can't risk having my plans traced back to me!"

Kevin grabs his change from a large glass canning jar that's sitting on his wooden dresser. He pours out about five dollars' worth of coins onto the dark orange bed spread, taking enough to ensure he has enough time to talk. The last thing Thomas wants is to be disconnected by the operator.

A sharp scheming mind tells the vengeful man he needs to hide the physical evidence that will directly link him to the crime he is to commit on Sauvie Island.

The powerful anxious suspended cop is swiftly walking on the uneven city sidewalk on a cold evening in his South East Portland Oregon neighborhood.

He is hustling in the light rain as a very cool breeze blows in his face to an enclosed telephone booth. It is located on the dimly lit east side next to a small convenient store's graffiti cinderblock wall without any windows.

In succession to perambulating in the night air for just over three blocks the metal and glass enclosed Bell coin operated phone is straight ahead.

Thomas steps in closing the door of the booth behind him, starts fishing out the notepad from his right back pocket of his blue jeans.

Kevin picks up the receiver then begins thumbing in two bucks worth of change into the shiny metal coin slot. He glances up and down at the small piece paper with the phone number written on it. Quickly

Hawk dials Josh Kinsky's number using his index finger to spin the chrome metal rotary dial clockwise making a jingling sound.

"I hope the guy knows a little more information than I do on the two gang's whereabouts right now!" Hawk ponders to himself while listening to the phone ring through the black plastic receiver.

"What's up?" A low dull sounding voice replies from the other end of the line.

"I'm looking for a Josh Kinsky!"

"You found him man. Who are you dude?"

"My name is Kevin Thomas, your brother Glenn used to work with my wife Linn at her leather shop."

Glenn's older brother pauses trying to figure out who this person is on the other end using his mind that is hazy from recently smoking a marijuana joint, "You're my younger brother's boss's husband the big cop. I think he said fellas on the street call you Blue Bird or something."

"Actually it's Blue Hawk but that name was not my doing what so ever! I'm sorry about Glenn he was a hard worker for my spouse."

"Thanks man, I am pretty bummed about my little brother's death, as you must about your wife being shot down where she stood Kevin! Anyway, what can I do for you?"

"Your brother told me that you may be able to help me find these sons of bitches that took our family members lives away from us!"

"Hey dude, I have a weird impression from the nature of this out of the blue jingle that you have given me, that you want to do more than arrest the bastards! Which I'm guessing you know are known Strangle Hold and Strife gang members."

"I do know who the perpetrators are that did the horrific deeds! What information do you have from the street on the dope dealing killers?"

"I have some info that is very useful to you, but I will tell you only on one condition man!"

"What's that Kinsky?"

"You let me go with you to pay these guys a visit. I want to do all of them like they did Glenn Blue Hawk!" Josh commences to sob as he tells Thomas his sentiments in a dark tone of voice.

"If I allow you to be a part of this special event you cannot tell any anybody not even your most trusted best friend in the world. I mean absolutely no one!" Thomas raises his voice emphasizing how serious the matter is to him on this life and death mission that is about to be embarked upon.

"Kevin I totally get the picture; I don't want to wind up in a state penitentiary doing twenty to life for doing something that is for the good of society man! Another thing I can do without is a hit out on me by drug dealers or possibly by you for running my big mouth!"

"I sense that we have an understanding with each other. Tell me all that you have stumbled upon from the inhabitants of the neighborhood around you?"

"What I caught wind of from my sources is that there is eight to twelve men hiding out at a farm house out in the country side north of town dude."

"Do you know where the farm house is located?"

"A peddler in the illegal drug market I once sold meth for told me an address of 1524 N Hemlock somewhere on Sauvie Island is where he heard they might be."

"Josh what you've given me has helped me fill in some blanks in my missing pieces." Kevin says in an upbeat tone into the pay phones mouth piece.

"When are we gunna hook up for the deed that is to be dealt out?" Josh asks.

"Stay close to the phone; I will be contacting you right after I talk to a buddy of mine." Thomas informs him; suddenly an automated operator chimes in, "Please deposit seventy five cents for seven more additional minutes."

"I have to make that call now Kinsky! I will talk to you later!" Hawk said then hangs up the phone before Josh could say a word in response.

The next call Thomas places is to a trust worthy person that he has been friends with since Vietnam. A kind of man that is able to provide the assistance that will make the operation go as smooth as a well-oiled machine.

Rapidly Hawk thumbs in additional money into the square metal box for the necessary person to person call. He dials up Sean Armstrong who was in his Ranger Platoon during the war that made it a full tour without even receiving a scratch from the South East Asian enemies.

After a year, Armstrong was accepted into the Green Berets where he carried out two more years. His special operations were throughout the country of Vietnam along with the Eastern side of Cambodia.

He was eventually shot on two separate occasions and stabbed once in a hand to hand combat incident against a wiry little Viet Cong soldier.

Sean took over running the family logging company his father started after his passing. His two younger brothers work with him on their one hundred and twenty nine acres of ever green trees.

"Hello!" A female voice says.

"Is Sean there?"

"Just a second, I'll get him for you."

"Who is it honey?" Armstrong asks as he opens a can of beer.

"I don't know. It's probably a timber faller who wants to have a drink with you or can't make it in to work tomorrow morning."

"You may be right and if it is the same guy as last week, I'm going to fire his ass!"

Thomas faintly hears over the phone, the conversation between Sean and his girlfriend Karen communicating with each other.

A few seconds later, Hawk hears, "This is Sean! What can I do this fine evening for ya!"

"It's Kevin! Are you too busy to talk to an old buddy?"

"What's going on partner?"

"I'm going to need a special favor from you, if you catch my drift."

"Let me go to the other phone in the bedroom." Armstrong hands the white telephone receiver to his girlfriend, "Put it back on the hook when I tell you I've picked up."

A few seconds later, Kevin hears his buddy yelling, "You can hang it up now!" A click sound comes through the line along with a door shutting. "OK Thomas, I now have a quiet private place to talk to at!"

"Some low life's shot and killed Linn at her down town business five days ago just before her closing time!"

"Damn it, I'm sorry to hear that! Do you have any idea who is responsible for murdering her?"

"It was four members of the Strangle Hold gang that murdered her according to the research that I've done. "At almost the same time four of Strife's members shot up my police cruiser skinning my head and hitting my bicep trying to take me out of equation!"

"How are you doing man?"

"I'm doing a little better! I can't believe that I'm about to ask you this question to you!"

"Please Thomas feel free to ask me anything that you have the conviction to, you probably could use a little help in your life right now my friend!"

"Remember you and I go back to the jungles in South East Asia. Heck we covered each other's backs on many occasions in that anarchy storm of a war!"

"I remember! What is it that you want from me?"

"I need you and the skills you possess to join me on a little hunting trip here in the great state of Oregon! Do you still have those AK 47 hunting rifles you showed me a while back at your place?" Kevin asks.

"Yes, I do still have those along with the several other weapons you have previously laid your eyes upon. Buddy there are lots of useful tools we can use on our expedition here at my place."

"So do you think we should go target shooting first to get the weapons sited in?"

"Nah I've got all the rifles sited in for accuracy, the only targets will be the unsuspicious prey. I can bring a couple of friends from my club; they are both construction contractors that are struggling for jobs right now. They will want to partake in a little field action to relieve some pinned up stress that has built up in their daily lives." Sean adds.

"I will be bringing a guy that wants to learn how to be a hunter Sean; it will be giving him great personal satisfaction to be a part of this get together."

"Make sure you keep the newby up under your wing out on the trail!" Armstrong exclaims.

"I'm glad that I can count on you for this friendly event among friends!"

"Believe me buddy it's going to be my pleasure to be part of a hunting trip once again. Hell I haven't shot a weapon in a few weeks any how Thomas!"

"Sean I have to hurry up and get off the phone; I got an operator telling me I have two minutes left until I have to deposit more change. Does around four or five tomorrow evening at your house work ok?"

"That sounds cool, I will be expecting to see you . . . . " The line went dead.

Kevin quickly slams the receiver down hanging it up on the vertical coin operated telephone. Almost instantly the tall muscular man fetches back the receiver plugging in around two dollars' worth of coins.

Rapidly he dials up Josh Kinsky up again, "You're in but you need to wear as many black articles of clothing, make sure you dress warm it's going to be a cold night. Do you know anywhere we can meet tomorrow at one besides your house that is?"

"There is a rundown vacant old lumber mill that has been shut down for six years. Parker's Wood Products its only five blocks from my pad man! Not to mention no body lives close to the vacant run down building dude!"

"Perfect, where exactly will you be standing tomorrow Kinsky?" Josh gives him detailed directions that will take Hawk to a huge gravel parking lot, "I will see you tomorrow, be on time Josh!"

That night Thomas is packing some of Linn's personal items in a big blue suitcase that's lying on his queen size bed. On the mattress is tall stack of clothing still on hangers that he is sorting when he comes across a leather jacket.

It is a tan suede leather jacket that his wife designed especially for him on her business's first production run of clothing. "There's no way I'm getting rid of this!" Kevin softly says out loud then somberly strolls back to the closet hanging up the sentimental article.

After finishing packing all of his deceased spouse's belongings folded nice and neat into the large travel bag, places it by the bedroom door so he won't forget it.

Ensuing a brief double check to make sure he has everything of Linn's that is to be taken to her home country, Hawk packs up a small brown suitcase for himself. He puts it beside the large blue luggage container.

Kevin gets out old bleach stained red sheet placing it on top of the comforter that is resting on his mattress. He removes his stainless steel Colt forty five auto from the night stand beside the bed that now seems cold as well as lonely.

Using the cleaning kit that Thomas purchased the same time as the police service handgun, he performs a thorough bore cleaning on the barrel. He scrubs, wipes and oils all of the moving parts within the weapon he has used as an important tool to uphold the law in Portland Oregon.

Upon putting the pistol back to a more proper working order a moment of clarity struck him while sliding the colt back into its black leather holster.

"I can't take my side arm! Shit, if I shoot it at the scene investigators will link me to the crime!" Kevin thinks to himself then promptly places it back where he has kept it for a number of years.

Hawk grabs a pair of black denim pants, a navy blue stocking hat, and other dark items of clothing tossing them into his green duffle bag. He is also bringing his trusty pair of black ten inch high leather combat airborne jump boots that served Thomas well in the Vietnam War.

Later that night the depressed man is tossing and turning in his big empty bed as his mind works on overtime. He is thinking about how he wishes the pretty Vietnamese young woman was still in his life along with what he is going to do to the scum that hurt her.

Kevin finally falls into a deep peaceful sleep traveling back in time where he and Linn were flying a large blue box kite on the sandy beach in Newport Oregon. It is a vivid wonderful dream that the warmth of the sun rays seem warm on his face as he looks to the sky.

There are many other people spread out with white strings that lead to colorful nylon flying vessels soaring to and fro in the powerful coastal breeze.

"Run sweetheart you can make it go higher! Just don't let it fall to the ground!" Linn excitedly shouts out to her sprinting husband with a red plastic spool that's feeding the thin string upward to the kite that is traveling to the beautiful cloudless atmosphere above them.

The young couple is comfortably dressed in tank tops, cotton shorts and inexpensive flip flops as they trod over the warm soft sand of the beach.

"Check it out dear; I've got it floating way up there! If it gets any further away I may have to get out my pair of binoculars to see it!" Kevin jokingly declares as he gazes over at his attractive young wife then followed by peering back up at the big baby blue flying device. It casually floats in the Pacific Coast's air sharing the sky with many soaring seagulls that lightly squawk.

"You are a kite controlling master my tall handsome husband who I love very much!"

"I love you too! Now get your tiny butt over here and take command of this crazy thing you wanted me to purchase from the kite maker's store!"

"I don't know sweetheart it will probably crash if I take line in my hand!" Linn tells him as she shyly walks a couple of steps in his direction.

"Come on honey, you'll just do fine. Besides I will stay right behind you the whole time."

"Oh, ok then!" she says then hurried to her husband who is handing the spool of string over so she can have a little fun with it as well.

The sun is burning big and bright where Linn has to squint even though she is wearing sun glasses as she peers up to see how the box kite fairing in the air.

His strong hands are on the petite brown skin woman's waist while he stands behind her as she tugs side to side on the string making it dance in the sky. She begins to laugh from the joy of playing around with their hovering toy.

In a flash the dream skips to when the pair are strolling together hand and hand close to the small white capped waves that crash on the wet sand to their left. They find a secluded spot on the seashore subsequent to beach combing picking up sea shells.

After a brief kiss, the loving couple stares out at the large choppy salt water of the vast Pacific Ocean as the warm sun shines on the two of them heating their bodies.

Gulls are flying above and landing around a hundred yards to the right of them on the coast's shore. Two commercial fishing boats are heading west off in the far distance in the semi calm aqua blue salt water.

The couple momentarily looks around at the enchanting natural sites that can be seen from where they are sitting on a long drift wood log.

A happy content Kevin can't help but stare at Linn as she smiles showing her white teeth looking ahead enjoying what she is viewing on a captivating summer day.

Noticing in the corner of her eyes, the beautiful woman rotates facing him. Looking deeply into his piercing blue eyes with her alluring dark brown eyes, "Kevin, I hope you stay with me forever!"

"You and I going to grow old together, have kids so we can have grandkids to spoil rotten."

They lean their bodies in close to each other to kiss. The passionate warm kissing is a warm wet sensation that is very intense.

An unexpected cold sensation comes over Thomas's lips along with non-response from the young lady he passionately loves.

Expeditiously he breaks free of the tight embrace to view his pale faced spouse with a lifeless empty gaze showing a blank expression. Linn's eyes are wide open no longer brown but now a dull grey color sunken deeper into her eye sockets.

A black hole is in the center of the once full of life young lady's pale colored forehead. Suddenly a copper bullet protrudes out of the opening falling freely to her small feet on the sand.

Crimson blood begins to lightly flow from the circular wound, Kevin's wife's mouth gapes open as if to take her final breath of life.

CHAPTER 11 _____

Waking up in a cold sweat, Thomas loudly hollers out, "Noooo! Nooo!" He rolls over in his queen size bed attempting to place his arm around Linn's warm body that is no longer with him. He starts patting the cold vacant spot where his once loving wife had once slumbered a very short time ago.

Exiting dream land, he comes to the sad realization that his young beautiful spouse is gone and he'll never get to lay his eyes on her kind lovely face again.

"Why God, why did Linn have to die?" He softly murmurs out loud lying on his back on top of the firm mattress. Thomas stares blindly into the morning darkness up to the ceiling above searching for answers from a higher power.

It is just prior to five am when Kevin gets out his lonely bed coming to the understanding that there is no possible way he is proceeding on with sleep.

Succeeding the realistic dream of Linn the career cop is experiencing another strong episode of sadness as well as loneliness. The one thing that keeps him from putting his pistol to his head is the firm desire to kill the scums that murdered his loving companion.

Kevin skips the normal routine of shaving after he hops out of the shower. Having a clean cut personal appearance is the last thing on the usually spit and polished man's mind.

Subsequent to a quick combing of his hair Hawk takes his as well as his wife's belonging to the Impala's trunk gently placing them inside.

Though Thomas doesn't feel like eating breakfast, he makes himself two good size pancakes to go with the large glass of orange juice he poured.

Kevin forces the food down his throat, knowing that he needs to keep his strength up for the event that is to take place that night.

That morning the emotionally distraught guy thoroughly tidies up the already fairly clean home prior to a real estate agent dropping by.

Thomas makes arrangements for the house he used to share with Linn to go on the market. He gives the sales woman a spare set of keys so she can begin showing the cozy structure to potential buyers while he is away.

Twenty minutes before one in the afternoon, Hawk travels to the closed down lumber mill to meet Josh in his red metallic two door vehicle.

A seriously appearing man is wearing aviator sunglasses to help conceal his identity along with the two days' worth of thick stubble showing. Hawk is almost starting to look like one of the thugs that hang out on the city's sidewalk hustling for cash.

At the mill the shaggy curly haired older brother of Glenn is loitering in the rough mud puddle clustered parking lot. Josh is taking a drag from a cigarette as he leans against a metal cyclone fence as he waits on the cold dark cloudy day.

Nervous acting Kinsky is dressed mainly in black excluding the dark blue denim jeans he has on that should blend well enough on a dark winter night.

Pulling the powerful sounding Impala to a spot in the gravel near Kinsky that is free of deep pot holes that are filled with muddy water.

Kevin stops the custom Chevy swiftly placing the car in park then leans across the seat rolling down the passenger side window, "Get a move on buddy!" He hollers out to the hippie dude that is a short span from the vehicle.

An annoyed Josh jerks open the passenger door, "Chill man, I'm right here dude!"

The ominous appearing Hawk doesn't say a word back just stares at him through mirrored sunglasses. A creeped out early twenties something male hurries into the Impala closing the car door.

Thomas instantly guns the accelerator sending rocks flying from both the wide rear tires, "Shit Blue Hawk you're on pins and needles about what we have to do today brother!" He exclaims gazing over at the unshaven wild acting man controlling the modified Chevrolet as if the world is closing in on him.

"Your information had better be right about where the gang's hideout is or your ass is mine!" Kevin speaks up and says while gazing over at his passenger.

"Man you don't need to sweat that at all! The dude that gave me the info is someone who knows things. Besides me and him go way back to when we were kids." Kinsky looks over at the much bigger man behind the steering wheel with a worried expression.

Obeying the posted speed limits, the pair cruise east through Portland to get to North East St. Helens Road for a straight shot north to Sauvie Island. They motor the city streets not saying a word to each other, Kevin leaves the car's radio off to collect his thoughts.

Thomas has a plan of action mapped out in his brain of the roads to take upon crossing the long Sauvie Island concrete bridge that crosses the Willamette River.

The night before he studied a map of the large island the bad guys are using as a refuge from justice that revealed every road documented by the state.

After journeying over the bridge, the two of them continues north on NW Sauvie Island Road in the direction of Strife's and Strangle Hold's hide away. On Hawk's left is the wide green river; off to the right are huge spreads of open agricultural fields.

Subsequent to traveling a few miles north Kevin starts making series of left and right turns on rural gravel roads that pass by numbers of old appearing farms.

It is a densely over casted afternoon which is a big plus for getting out for a surveillance detail without being noticed easily.

"According to the map that I read Hemlock Road is just ahead of us running north and south. If that's true then the farm house is roughly a total of four miles from where we are driving now."

Stopping the vehicle shutting the engine off on the shoulder of the road, Hawk takes his powerful binoculars out from under his black bucket seat.

He takes them out of their case then places the large field glasses up to his eyes peering through the Impala's windshield.

Though the sign is a good two hundred meters from where they are parked it appears to be right in front of him as he views Hemlock. The green metal sign that is spelled out with white letters on the galvanized pole is an uplifting sight for Kevin.

"So is it the same street that I told you the other night over the wire dude?"

"It certainly looks that way Josh!"

"Cool, which direction do we go in man?"

"The map in my head is coming to an end, reach in to the glove compartment and fetch out a white piece of paper that I wrote on."

"Ah here it is! Looks like you decided to make your own chart to get us there."

"Just hand it to me!" Hawk snatches it from the hippies held up hand.

Studying the home made graph that he drew out with a blue ball point pen on his dining room table the previous night at his house. Thomas moves his index finger over the wrinkly note book paper while Kinsky looks on beside him.

"We'll make a right turn on Hemlock follow it south for about two and half miles before the road makes a right turn for remainder of just over a mile. So we're going to have to park this loud machine long before we get close to where the gang members are located."

"Sounds like the two of us will be hoofing it in to catch a closer glimpse of the farm place dude."

"You got it Kinsky!" Hawk said prior to starting the powerful V8 engine up again.

Turning on Hemlock Street they drive two hundred meters before coming to a rusty metal mailbox on the left side of the rough rural road.

It read 1380 N. Hemlock in faded weathered paint that the resident used a one inch paint brush to write out many years ago. The good size beige farmhouse is at least a quarter of a mile down a wide driveway with a huge yellow sheet metal pole barn on the far right of the home.

Next to the metal building that is full of farm equipment is a vast field every bit of three hundred acres in size. When in season it used for rows of tall stalks of sweet corn that the farmer sells to an Oregon Cannery.

Continuing south there is corn fields on both sides of the gravel road for around half a mile before coming to orchards full of various fruit trees.

Brush along with tall black berry briars are growing over aging barbed wire fences on both sides of the gravel street they travel on. The over growth of plant life that people don't maintain help serve as natural barriers along the private properties.

Close to a quarter of a mile ahead Hawk sees the road turn the corner to the west, he knows that the homestead he is searching for is less than two miles away.

Slowly cruising along, the suspended cop observes a wide open space that leads down off the road. The graveled opening in the thick foliage use to serve as a driveway to a home that burnt down many years earlier. Now there is only a concrete foundation in the middle of brown dirt beside a broad tree line of Ash, Alder, and Cotton wood trees.

"Oh this is going to work perfect!" Kevin comments as he pulls in the wide gravel driveway with the slight downward incline.

Thomas applies the parking brake while remaining on the entrance's rocky slope leery about the condition of the property's soil ahead.

Leaving the car the running, Hawk gets out investigating how soft the dirt is beyond the rocked ground he parked upon. Light patches of multiple colors of leaves of several different sizes and shapes clustered the brown earth.

Josh follows Kevin's lead stepping out of the Chevrolet strolling to where the tall man is using his right foot to test the softness of the earth's soil.

"Think you'll get your ride's tires stuck here man?"

"Kinsky my friend we're in luck, the dirt is surprisingly as hard as a rock. Plus my Impala has traction bars that aid both back wheels to spin simultaneously."

"Right on Thomas, I'll wait here if you want to rotate your machine down here!"

"Now you're thinking buddy. Watch your toes so they don't get run over!"

Kevin drives his vehicle over the ground with ease not spinning his tires what so ever, just steadily cruising to the tree line on the left.

He turns his red Sedan around then backs it up between two tall trees in a space wide enough to fit a vehicle beside his Chevy. His car is perfectly concealed by trees and brush so passersby using Hemlock Road won't view it.

Kinsky is next to the driver's side door by the time Hawk exits the vehicle with his high powered binoculars around his thick muscular neck.

"Do you want me to wait with the Chevy or come with you man?"

"Here's the deal, you will be partnered up beside me tonight on what is to go down! Of course I want you to come along with me, basically right now marks the starting point of the mission at hand!"

"Cool, I was hoping you'd say yes! I really don't want to be left out of anything dude!" Josh expresses with excitement showing in his voice.

"Follow me, keep your voice down and watch where you step so you won't create any noise. Last thing the two of us need is to be spotted by one of those ass holes before we get a chance to make it back with our weapons!"

The pair swiftly walk south in the dense tree line until they begin to see the tall grassy pasture. Noisy birds chirp throughout the narrow forest as the cool wind blows in the branches high above their heads.

Both men stepped over a small fallen tree just previous to hiking west on the surveillance quest. If Kevin's geological studies are accurate the murdering drug dealer's hideout is straight ahead on the right somewhere around a mile.

Ensuing hoofing it in the brushy tree line for close to a two mile span, a big white two story old farm house comes into Hawk sight.

He stops without taking another step; utilizing both large hands Thomas lifts the field glasses to his blue eyes. Acquiring a peek through the big black binoculars, Kevin realizes the distance is to great clearly make out the numbers on the mailbox in front of the house.

"Do you see anything?" Josh asked after Kevin places the view glasses down.

"No, I'm trying to get a glimpse of the address that is on the rusty old mail box that is on the shoulders of the gravel street on the left side of the farms unpaved drive way."

"Dude is it the right place or not?"

"Gosh dang it, I can't see diddly squat from this location. Part of the metal box is covered by thorny black berry bushes that are growing next to the numbers on one side." Kevin exclaims.

Without saying another word the suspended cop begins jogging west for a better view of the home's address that's over a gap of a quarter mile.

Josh ends up having to run to catch back up with the athletically built man who restlessly strides along. His feet are moving at a fast pace as he maneuvers his body between the various clusters of plant life.

Upon finding a good point to look from Hawk peers with the aid of the binoculars from the cover of the tree line. He discovers from the rusty mailbox that it is indeed the address he has been searching for.

The out of shape drug user is bent over standing stationary as he clutches his right side tightly trying to comfort himself from a painful side ache.

He is also breathing hardest doing his darnest to suck in a sufficient amount of air into his bad lungs. "Smoking those two packs of cigarettes for seven years has taken the toll on me man!"

"Are you going to make it buddy?"

"I, I'll, whoo be alright Kevin. Give me a second please." Josh says muttering out words as he gasps for breaths.

"I would hate to have you die on me in advance of a single shot even being squeezed off at the dirt bags."

"You don't have to worry me about dying now! I want them to die too much to let that happen dude!"

"Good news my long haired friend, I have just confirmed by using my sneak peeks over yonder there. It is the correct farm house according the address on the ancient mail box."

"Dude are you dead serious about that Kevin! Did you see any of the gang members?"

Hawk steps to a better sight beside a wide cotton wood tree to once again utilize the high powered field glasses he brought with.

He peers across the wide field to the white two story century old farmhouse that has a huge red barn one hundred meters southwest to the rear.

A nervous Kinsky stands close behind the much bigger man as he watches across the 250 plus meter span to the large Victorian Style home.

"I can see the barrels of two rifles leaning on a forty angle sticking out of the window in front of the house, with two thugs sitting on chairs as some kind of look out or something Josh." Kevin informs while removing the large black binoculars from his eyes holding them chest level with both of his hands.

"Are they Strife or Strangle Hold fellas?"

"By the way they are dressed along with their ethnicity; I would have to say they're not associated with them."

"It looks like a couple of figures heading toward the barn dude!"

Hawk quickly brings the binoculars up to his face again looking to the weathered barn with the two wide open doors. "The couple of dudes that I see as far as I can tell is skinny leader Jimmy Bloodgood on the left with the long straight brown hair. A much stockier fella with the crew cut hair cut and the huge arms that are full of tattoos is definitely with one of the Portland gangs. Here, maybe you'll recognize the big guy on the right."

Without hesitation Josh grabs the large viewing device quickly looking through, "Yep that's certainly Stuart, I've seen him wearing that black leather vest with the dragon spitting out fire on the back many times Blue Hawk!"

Each gang leader takes hold of a red wood door looking around paranoid prior to pulling it shut behind them as they enter in the building.

Thomas took mental notes of every single detail he observes, planning out every detail for the surprise attack. He plots in the same fashion as if he was still an Army Ranger about to partake on a night operation in a squad.

"Let's hit the highway to my buddies place. We have to start drawing out tactics for the surprise party for the bunch of thugs on the other side of the road."

"I love the crazy way you put words into sentences! You crack me up man!" Josh exclaims as he perambulates a short distance behind Kevin!"

CHAPTER 12 _____

Succeeding making it back to the parked Chevy, Kevin sits down in the driver's seat shutting the door. "You seem a bit tense right now. Pay attention to what you're shown and told as well as have confidence in yourself! I feel you'll do fine if you follow my advice."

Kinsky is seated on the passenger's side staring at Hawk while he listens intently to what had to say. Josh doesn't utter a word even after the man he considers the leader started the vehicle driving them away.

Silence helps the off duty police officer think of many different tactical methods that could be used in the coming event.

Crossing the wide Columbia River traveling on the long concrete bridge that leads to state of Washington, Kevin flicks on the radio. He has the factory deck in the Chevrolet's dashboard tuned to his favorite rock n roll station.

"Maybe if I turn up some good tunes we'll both relax a little during our road excursion." They are listening to music coming from a single speaker that is in the middle of the light brown dash.

Kevin and his shaggy haired passenger shared casual conversation at times during the trip to Sean Armstrong's residence in the hills.

A strong heavy rain suddenly comes on while Thomas tries maintaining a constant speed of sixty five as the two of them journey north on the freeway. There is a moderate amount of traffic on Interstate five as the asphalt begins to have a layer of standing water.

Just past Vancouver Washington, the close rural surrounding towns become the scenic sites of small look-alike mill communities.

Upon making a right at exit fifty seven to begin heading east off of the traffic filled freeway. They travel by a large truck stop full of tractor trailer trucks that is just off I-5.

Now on State Highway 503 the pair has tall evergreen trees on both sides on the two lane road. Galvanized steel guard rails protect on turns at times from steep drop offs as Hawk powers up the winding road.

"Dude scope it out up ahead two deers man!" Kinsky excitedly informs out lout as he leaned forward pointing ahead with his index finger.

Off in the distance, Josh sees a pair of black tail does and trailing close to the rear of them a much smaller fawn. All three are scampering fast across the road a fair gap from where they are traveling. The deer run down a muddy bank into the trees that lead to a small flowing creek below.

"When you have more than one deer they are still referred as deer not deers."

"Who cares what they are called Hawk? How much further is it to your buddies place?"

"From here it is just over three miles."

Subsequent to driving a little over two more miles, Thomas turns left off of 503 onto a narrow gravel road that leads directly to Armstrong's house.

It is a steep rocky driveway which twists and turns as it makes it way to his friend's property high above. Kevin has to place the Impala's automatic transmission part way up the hill until the ground starts plateauing off.

Coming into view is Sean's dark grey double wide mobile home; a gapped distance to the left is his large wood constructed shop.

Thomas checks his wrist watch seeing that it is four o' nine that afternoon as he cruises closer to where his buddy's brown 4x4 Ford pickup.

To the left of Armstrong's crew cab F350 is a metallic blue four wheel blazer which Hawk realizes probably belongs to one of the men Sean knows.

Kevin and Josh get out of the sixty five Impala at the same time. Looking around they see Sean and two other men strolling out from the large shop toward them close to fifty yards away.

"Geeze Hawk those dudes are some of the roughest looking fellas I have ever laid my eyes on in my life!"

"They do have a muscular macho appearance that gives you an outward impression of if you get in our way you will be pounded into the dirt."

As the three get closer, Kevin sees that the Caucasians Vietnam vets are dressed in green cargo pants and combat boots. Two of them are wearing OD green tee shirt while Sean has on a short sleeve black cotton on.

"Looks like you made up here buddy!" Armstrong states as he comes closer.

"Man I'll tell you it wasn't exactly easy on that driveway of yours!" Thomas replies shaking Sean's hand.

"I want to introduce you to a couple of dependable men starting with this big guy to my left. This scary dude is Clive Nagely he was in my company when I went into the Green Berets Nam."

"Nice to meet you Clive, Kevin Thomas!" He says shaking the much bigger man's hand.

The six foot six ex Green Beret with the thick auburn beard and long ponytail gave Hawk a firm handshake that almost hurt.

"Hi I'm Alan Steele! How's it going?" said an average built man with black curly hair and an overgrown handle bar mustache steps up then shook his hand.

"Steele here was a Navy Seal sniper, he along with Nagely are part of the Militia I have been trying to get you to join for years."

"Maybe someday I'll join. You never know right. Anyhow this is Josh Kinsky. He doesn't have our background but he has a damn good reason to takeout the scum tonight!"

"We've got a little time this afternoon to square Kinsky away a bit. Plus Thomas, he's got you tonight as experienced battle buddy to lead him in the fight!"

Hawk can't help but notice that Sean's beard is a lot longer than it was the last he seen him previously six months ago while he thinks to himself. "They look more like bikers than clean cut soldiers."

An uneasy much smaller Josh steps toward them shakes the three war Veterans hands quietly saying, "It is nice to meet you!"

"Come on in gentleman have a bite to eat along with a couple of beers! We'll talk about things for a few in my nice toasty warm house."

"Sounds like a great plan to me Armstrong!" Steele says.

"Let's hit it boys!" Nagely added.

"I want to get my gear out of the trunk of my car first; I'll catch up with you gents in a second!" Kevin says while motioning to the rear of the Sedan.

Hawk turns the key opening up the wide trunk lid as a tense Josh Kinsky pulls out a pack of generic cigarettes. His thin boney hand snatched the half empty container from his small upper right hand coat pocket. The scruffy haired guy's shaky hand lights his stick of tobacco sending a white smoke plume into the cold air.

"Smoke em up now Kinsky cause tonight hoofing in the darkness, no fire from a lighter or glow from a cigarette cherry will be happening! We are not going to have those dirt bags see us before we begin exterminating them one by one!"

"Not burning a weed to kill the bastards that snuffed out my little brother won't be a problem for me what so ever man!" He replies after taking a long drag.

A light drizzle starts falling from the sky as Hawk tugs out his green canvas duffle bag up from the open trunk. "Come on slim let's get you something in your belly! Believe me you're going to need it for tonight!" Kevin leads the way to his army buddy's spacious factory built home.

Thomas ambulates casually through the open front door with the big gym bag draped over his right shoulder, "Please have a seat with the others in the living room, I'm grabbing beers for everyone! I hope that's going to work for you all!" Sean speaks up from the kitchen area on Hawks right hand side so everybody could hear.

"Sounds great buddy, I'm going change into my night attire in your bathroom."

"Go for it, you know where the head is."

Thomas figured it was as a good time as any to switch into the battle clothing he was to wear during the surprise attack on the drug dealing gangs.

"Hey Armstrong, I would rather have a cup of coffee if you've got any!" Clive's deep voice hollers out from the other side of the room as Kevin is walking away.

"Don't you know coffee will stunt your growth buddy!" Sean said like the true smart aleck he can be following strolling closer to the living room looking to his large friend seated on the dark brown sofa.

"That's why I drink the wonderful black liquid; I don't want to get any taller than my six foot six height that I'm at right now!"

Good one Nagely, I have a pot of coffee that's still on and you're very welcome to polish it off big fellow. I'll bring a hot cup of java to you with the beers." Armstrong informs prior to rotating around heading back to the kitchen to play the role of a good host.

In succession to putting on his dark clothing he briskly walks his bag full of casual his Chevrolet. The precipitation coming down is much heavier now as he tosses the duffle into the spacious cavity then slammed the trunk shut.

Hawk notices Sean is opening the entrance door of the manufactured home to be polite in a snide fashion while peering outside, "Hey, you chuckle head come out of the nasty rain before you melt!"

"This is the Pacific Northwest hardcore warrior we'll all be more than likely soaked to the bone when we're out on Sauvie Island tonight."

Sean is standing in the open doorway with a twelve ounce can of Budweiser gripped in his right hand, "Thank you for your wonderfully kind gesture Armstrong!" The suspended cop remarks as he is doing his famous wild eyed psychotic face when he passes his friend without a single blink.

This is the same facial appearance Kevin exhibited years before in the Army barracks in Vietnam to help relieve pinned up stress.

"Bring that attitude this evening Blue Hawk and you'll show those gang bangers that they messed with one crazy son of a bitch that means business!"

Entering the residence Kevin pivots back facing his Vietnam buddy displaying a confused look, "How did you know about my street nickname from Portland?"

"Your fellow Oregonian over there told us that folks on the Northeast side of your city refer to you by that title."

Thomas slowly turns toward Josh who is sitting by himself on a flower patterned love seat appearing a bit sheepish from over hearing the conversation.

Hawk briefly shakes his head as he feels a bit annoyed by the blabber mouth as he speaks out loud, "Thanks a lot Kinsky now I'm going to have Sean here calling me Hawk for the rest of my life."

"You got that right Hawk!" Armstrong declares before taking a sip out of his beer.

Sorry Thomas it just slipped out when I was casually conversing dude!" The shaggy haired young man explained before Kevin took a seat on the vacant lavender padded armchair across from him.

"Don't sweat it Josh, I've had a lot of worse nicknames thrown my way!" He says while cracking open the Budweiser that Sean just handed him.

A more at ease Kinsky starts to loosen up talking more as he takes a drink once in a while from his cold can of domestic lager beer.

"I'm done being the hostess so if any of you needs another beer your free to grab one from the fridge. There is a large kettle of stew warming up on the burner that I've been stirring off and on that everyone is welcomed to get a bowl of when I find out its hot."

"Let's not suck down so much suds that we're drunk, we need to keep clear heads for our mission coming up!" Alan Steele states sitting on the couch beside Clive.

Everybody agreed by either verbally speaking up or nodding their head in approval of what the sniper sincerely expressed as he glanced around to everyone.

"Before I forget to tell you all, I just want to say how thankful I am for the help that will be given to the objective that is to be achieved soon!"

"Hell, I think I speak for all of us when I say it is truly our pleasure Thomas to pay these jerks back for their deed!"

"We would want the same thing to transpire if one of our loved ones was murdered by bunch of dirt bags!" Nagely speaks from the heart previous to standing up making his way for a refill in the white coffee cup he is using.

"Anyway Kevin have you spoken with my law abiding cousin Chad?"

"Surprisingly enough Chad he is the lead detective from our precinct that is assisting with the murders in Linn's leather shop."

"What did my cousin find out from investigating the case so far?" Sean inquires after wiping the lager that dribbled from the can's opening. It happened when he took a large drink from his beer ending up in his thick black beard.

"After picking his brain the only tangible evidence he had was the calibers of the firearms that were used at my wife's business. What Chad knew for sure was that the Strife gang was involved in ambushing me, because I left two of them dead in a car."

"At this juncture I'm guessing the cop known as Blue Hawk found out on his own who were responsible parties that killed his beautiful spouse!" Armstrong says getting up to go to the kitchen to stir the food on the stove not giving Kevin a chance to answer the question. He already has enough insight to guess his Army buddy went to the street for his answers.

The conversation lightens up following Sean exiting the living room area. Four remaining men changed gears by talking about College Football games.

"Stews ready, so I suggest fetching a bowl of grub while it's hot! Times a ticking I just shut the burner off boys!" Armstrong says when he comes back in the room carrying a ceramic bowl of steaming food.

Simultaneously the hungry men take their friend's advice going to the kitchen to get some of his girlfriend's home made vegetable beef stew.

Sean turns on the portable radio on the in table next to the chair he is seated in. It begins playing country music which is the style the logging contractor has listened to since he was a young boy.

CHAPTER 13 _____

Kevin eats his meal not paying much attention to the music that is playing in the room. Not a lot is said among the five of them as they dig into their food. Alan is the first to finish his stew, he quietly sings along to a Willie Nelson song upon taking the empty bowl to the kitchen sink.

"I haven't heard the precise number that the five of us are going against on Sauvie Island." Nagely says upon returning back from the other room.

"A guy I used hang out with told me that there will be maybe as many as twelve dudes." Josh informs the much larger man seated close by him then uses both of his hands to brush his long brown hair behind his ears.

"Sounds like a durable number if we properly utilize our trained skills swiftly as well as accurately in the dark of the night." Steele added.

"Why did Kinsky here want to join this little get together you've assembled Thomas?" Clive asked while staring at Josh without trust.

"Those scum bags murdered my younger brother in cold blood leaving him for dead on the floor where he worked!" An angry Josh Kinsky responded glaring back at the big man losing all his fear from the rage that erupted.

"I'm sorry, I didn't know about your relative!" Nagely sincerely explained looking the tearing eyed young man in the face.

Kinsky doesn't say a word in response, just sits in silence wiping the tears out of his brown eyes. "I'd break out the bong to smoke some good high grade marijuana but there is a police officer in the room. The last thing I want is to have Karen come home from work tonight and find a note saying that Officer Blue Hawk has arrested me for pot." Sean says while smiling from ear to ear with his arms out in front of him as if his wrists were handcuffed together.

Everybody laughs except Thomas who waits until the laughter quiets to a low point before making his come back, "Hell ya I would cuff him and stuff him to protect one of us from being shot! He's dangerous enough with a loaded rifle when he's sober let alone when he's stoned on mind altering loco weed!"

Everyone in the living room is laughing hard after the comment including Sean who is slapping the arm of his recliner chair while busting up.

Kevin moves back his sleeve glancing at his military wrist watch noticing the time is already five thirty three in the evening. "All fun aside we need to start preparing for the night operation that's closing in on us!"

"When will your girlfriend will be coming home tonight Sean?" Alan asked after looking at the clock that is mounted on the wall.

"She doesn't get off work until after the Elk tavern closes at two thirty in the morning. I can take a hint guys, grab your beers and follow me to my shop!"

Each of them quickly get to their feet anxious to start planning what is to happen for their friends hiding out at the hundred year old farm.

Subsequently to exiting his war buddy's home, Kevin notices the rain has stopped along with the sun setting to end the day. It is causing the clouds in the sky to glow a bright red color which is pleasing to the eyes.

Following a brisk shuffle down the front porch steps, Thomas pauses for a moment. He takes the time to admire the breath taking view of the vast Washington forest of dark green pine trees.

"A gorgeous site isn't it Hawk, I have not tired from gazing out at the view on nice days since I've moved up here buddy!" Sean declares while standing next to his taller friend.

"Hey Hawk I've got the map out from the glove compartment man!" Josh yells over the roof of the Impala prior to slamming the passenger door shut.

"Come on you two nature lovers we got a plot to draw out to do ourselves some killing this fine evening!" Alan impatiently hollers out wanting to get started with the necessary attack plot.

Both men stop peering out and swiftly get a move on toward the large site built shop. "Hurry up Armstrong, Blue Hawk move your skinny ass's men!" Clive hollers out standing with the other two next to the wide metal garage door that is closed and locked up tight.

"Great now you have the giant calling me the cartoon bird name!" Thomas says glancing at Armstrong as they both go into a light jog.

"Hey, I can't help it if the name suits you to a tee my friend!" Sean states grinning!

At the shop, Armstrong takes out his keys from his front pants pocket while everyone stands around him waiting to get in. He unlocks the door handle lock prior to turning the key in the heavy duty grey metal door's deadbolt.

After entering the big building Thomas sees a walk-in gun vault in the far right corner of the room with the thick steel combination lock door shut.

In the middle area there is a round table with a two foot by three foot white blank sheet of paper on the surface along with writing utensils. There are no chairs in sight for anybody to sit on. "Do you know what we're dealing with Hawk?" Clive asks.

"Yes I do, I drew a map on how to get there."

"Here's the chart you drew out Hawk!" Josh says handing him the small piece of paper."

"Kevin have you already took a good look at the farm house as well as everything surrounding the home itself?" Armstrong asks.

"I thoroughly checked it out!"

"Draw out in better detail what you have scribbled on your small piece of paper Thomas. We'll use what you map out to lay out our course of action."

"You got it Sean, just like the old days!"

Drawing using a yellow number two pencil Hawk creates a visual pictorial of the Sauvie Island farm along with the immediate surroundings of the property.

He charts everything out as the men are standing behind and beside the tall guy that's bent over sketching on the large sheet of paper.

The off duty police officer's map doodles is almost as good as a professional artist, "Damn you draw as good as Sean!" Clive says after the map was completely finished.

"Gather in close and listen up Thomas is going to explain everyone's role along with the by the numbers plan that is to be followed out tonight!" Sean speaks up saying with great authority.

"Let's all synchronize our watches to precisely time out the engagement on the low lifes!" Steele says.

The four other men go off the mark of Alan's black Swiss made diver's watch that he purchased on the black market in Thailand.

"I'm not wearing a wrist watch right now!" Josh nervously explains.

"Don't worry about it little buddy, your time keeper is going to be Mister Thomas." Nagely said patting Kinsky lightly on the back.

"From what Armstrong's filled me in on you Steele, is that your job in the Navy seals was a sharp shooting sniper on spec ops."

"Yes that is correct Thomas!" Alan crisply responds.

"My understanding is that you have a rifle that has a mounted scope on it that Steele can use Armstrong."

"The only long range weapon that I have that will fit the bill is a camouflage bolt action three hundred magnum that was once used to hunt elk. It is equipped with a custom silencer and a mounted high powered scope on it; I paid a pretty penny to obtain it a while back."

"Three hundred mag is a high velocity round that will pass through a human body like a hot knife traveling through warm butter!" States Nagely looking at Sean.

"What is the estimated distance of the intended targets, where I am to be placed at?"

"I figure less than two hundred meters from your stealth position in the dense tree line Steele. Earlier today I viewed two thugs on the second floor by both upstairs windows, they must be the main lookouts.

They appeared to be armed with M-16 rifles while facing Hemlock Road." Kevin informs as he points with his index finger to the drawing on the large map he created.

"Hawk it will be my absolute pleasure viewing a couple of turds of society drop as they lose their lives from my full metal Jacket bullets!" The ex-Navy Seal replied showing a big white grin after speaking.

"Here's the order of how I'm going to have it play out under the cold night's sky in the country side! First of all our Seal sniper is going to peer across to the property taking out anybody that is in his cross hair. He'll do that previous to anyone setting foot outside our heavy foliage cover." Kevin explains giving the low down calling the shots to his eager followers who are looking for answers.

"Where exactly do you want me?" Nagely impatiently asks the man in charge.

"I want you and your sidekick Armstrong to flank left encompassing to the rear of the old farm house. You two will be going to the big red barn eliminating any opposing gang members at the site."

"So I take it you and Josh will be hiding in the trees while my two man team is busy kicking ass."

"Not quite! Kinsky and I will more than likely will be taking on more guys than you when we strike the home!"

"That's just great man! My very first hit and I have a bunch of dudes to deal with Hawk!" A frustrated Josh openly expressed.

"It will be a walk in the park on a beautiful sunny day for you little guy!" Clive says right before chuckling.

"Approximately one minute after you both leave Sean, we will snake our way to the front door of the hideout. A surprise forced entry from my team will get the ball rolling for tonight's festivity." Kevin states as he looks everyone in the eyes while speaking from the heart.

"Absolutely the sooner the two hoods armed with the sixteen's are removed the safer you two will be making your way to the front of the farms property." Sean chimes in seeing eye to eye with Thomas's decision for the sniper's course of action.

Alan nods in agreement while carefully listening absorbing the information that dictates the role he is to perform against the Strife and Strangle Hold organizations.

Subsequent to going over exactly what everyone is to do step by step at length, as well as evaluating the drawn diagram, Armstrong opens the gun vault.

The ex-Green Beret has all the men wait outside the safe while he retrieves each rifle. He hands Steele his high powered .30 caliber bolt action rifle he is to utilize from a distance away.

Kevin and Josh each receive a Chinese manufactured AK–47 assault rifle that is very dependable in the field. Armstrong decides his two man team will be using automatic SKS automatic weapons.

"My fully automatic weaponry rarely jams up, that is why I own them instead of M-16's. The one I used in Vietnam a few years ago double fed rounds way too often!" Armstrong says while holding his SKS waist level in his two hands.

Sean gives everyone brief instructions on how to handle the weapon in a safe efficient manner even though most of them were very familiar with machine guns.

He is a by the numbers kind of a teacher, the style developed after serving as a drill sergeant at Fort Benning Georgia. Armstrong was honorably discharged from Benning following full filling the contract he rejoined to complete because the Army was short of instructors at the time.

A refresher course is only going to make what they are about to that much smoother. Having a slick fluent mission is the sentiment among the men as they patiently listen to what is told to them.

"After I slap in a fully loaded magazine, then what do I do man?" Kinsky asked looking confused.

"Give me your weapon and I'll show you one on one again how to pull back on the bolt lever!" Sean replied feeling a bit annoyed by the ignorant hippy that didn't pay enough attention the first time.

Kinsky is new at the game that is soon to be played out under the evening's dark cloudy sky. Josh has only shot his own stainless steel three fifty seven magnum revolver.

He used to carry the four inch barreled handgun when he was dealing illegal drugs on the north east streets of Portland Oregon.

For a dude playing the role of a street wise tough guy Josh doesn't have a lot of experience in handling fire arms or in fact putting a bullet into a human being's body.

"All of my rifles have a number engraved on the left side of the wood stock. Please gentlemen remember what number is yours; I want to see each of my beloved pieces of destruction back in its sequestered spot!" Armstrong lays down the law as he peers intently into each of their faces while he speaks with candor in his spacious shop.

"Since the rifle I am to use is the only one that is a three hundred magnum bolt action. Not to mention that it has a big Leupold scope mounted on it, I will be able to tell it's mine a little easier Armstrong."

"Hell, that is precisely why Sean gave you that long range weapon to play sniper with Allen my boy! "Teases Nagely as he jokingly pats the smaller size man on top of his head.

"It just so happens to be the number one reason why I chose to give him that rifle to use, followed by a close second that Allen Steele is a quintessential sharp shooter." Sean states then exhibits a smirk on his lips after the smart ass comment directed back to Clive.

Thank you Armstrong, I guess buddy! Responds back Steele glancing toward Sean feigning a goofy puzzled appearance on his face as he makes light with his militia buddies.

"Well gents as of now it's not very late but it certainly has grown plenty dark outside." Thomas mentions subsequent to a quick glimpse at his military style wrist watch.

The hands read ten minutes past seven that edgy winter night that everyone could hardly wait to get on with. "Shit partner, should we beat feet to start the task that has to be dealt with tonight old friend?" Sean inquires to Kevin.

Hawk is standing next to his close Army buddy by the now securely locked up dark grey steel vault door. "Good Lord the earlier we get started the better for me Armstrong; I have a red eye flight in the morning out of the Portland International Airport to Ho Chi Minh City South Vietnam!"

"People let's put it in gear now! Place the rifles I have provided you with neatly into the box so we can head off my beautiful mountain to kick some serious low life ass!" Sean said showing great enthusiasm as he spoke up loudly to motivate everyone to start moving.

There is a long narrow aluminum tote box that's painted olive drab green in true Army fashion. Its hinged lid is swung open as it rests on the cold smooth finished concrete floor seven feet from the raised garage door that leads outside.

All the fire arms as well as the many rounds of ammunition that are to be used that night are intended to be stored in the metal container. It is to be placed in the bed of Sean's four wheel drive pickup for transport to Sauvie Island.

"Armstrong the AK-47's that you're letting me and Kinsky borrow can go in the trunk of my Impala, since I will be leading the way to the fixed starting point!" Hawk explains gazing his friend in the eye with a determined look of meaning business clearly showing in his demeanor.

"That idea is more than fine with me Thomas; just don't get pulled over by one of your brothers in blue!"

"Thanks Sean, come on Josh you can put your weapon in my car! Make sure that automatic rifle's switch is placed on the safety position slim or you're liable to blow your damn skinny foot off before you lay eyes on a bad guy!" Hawk speaks up saying previous to double checking the locked and loaded ready for action AK-47 for it being set on safe.

Kevin hears the distinct metallic sound of the shaggy hair young man flicking it into the safe position on the deadly machine gun. "It is on safe now Hawk!" Kinsky hollers out as he briskly strides to catch up to the vengeful cop a short distance ahead of him in the darkness.

"Did you grab an extra thirty round magazine of full metal jacket rounds for your automatic rifle soldier?" Hawk asks walking now beside the inexperienced younger guy already knowing the answer long before inquiring. "I didn't think I needed to snatch one up when I was back there at the shop!" Josh replied back as he swiftly perambulates on Kevin's left side.

They are making their way across the muddy ground that squishes below the pair's leather boots while blindly hurrying in the darkness.

"I got you covered Josh for bullets not that we're necessarily going to require any more than thirty rounds a piece. As for myself, I would rather have them and not need than be the other way around discovering I'm in a bad way!

Kinsky finding out I am in trouble for lack of preparation is what I personally don't want to have happen!" "Good point sergeant Thomas sounds like a good philosophy to live by man!"

CHAPTER 14 _____

Upon reaching Kevin's two door sedan Blue Hawk fumbles about searching for the proper key to unlock the Chevrolet's spacious rear compartment. "Ah there the little devil is!" Once the lid is popped open the tiny light bulb illuminates the automobile's deep cavity.

Kevin pushes his luggage and green bag forward to set the pair of automatic rifles flat on the trunks inner surface. Seeing his dearly missed wife's personal belongings he neatly packed in a true caring sense in one travel suitcase caused a sick feeling in the pit of his stomach.

Thomas's mood swiftly changes from sadness to anger as he stands gazing into the open space at Linn's things. He doesn't even notice Armstrong, Steele, and Nagely standing quietly in the shadows behind him.

Hawk unscrews the tiny light bulb that's attached to the trunk lid to eliminate any unwanted illumination when he parks in the tree line area.

"Hope you're ready to do some killing cause I am more than ready to for a little pay back tonight Kinsky!" Kevin monotonically utters leaning over the Chevy's spacious compartment.

"Shit soldier, we're all set to do a mission of night extermination Hawk!" Alan chimes back enthusiastically, expressing what each of the war veterans felt at the time.

Kevin throws a couple of small old blankets over the two AK-47's lying parallel with each other to conceal the powerful pair of weapons just before closing the lid. He slowly turns facing his fellow vigilantes that are a few feet from where he is standing.

"Start rolling down the road in your hot rod Thomas, myself accompanied by my two amigos will be a short distance to the ass end of your Impala!"

"Alright then Armstrong, let's do this then!" Hawk says just before making his way to the driver's side door quickly pulling it open in hopping behind the wheel.

Steele and Nagely each grab a metal handle of the weapons case that is set down on the wet gravel surface. They start caring it once again to the tall four door crew cab pickup truck that Sean purchased brand new a year earlier.

The returning trip to the farm land on Sauvie Island seemed to take an extremely long amount of time for the anxious suspended cop.

It took all the self-control that Hawk could muster not to drive a great deal faster than the posted speed limit signs on the shoulder of the road.

Rock & roll music played way down low on the factory Chevrolet deck that lit up a pretty green color in the unlit interior of the vehicle.

Many military strategy scenarios played out in Thomas's vengeful brain of what he might do to quickly take out the band of hiding scum.

Going after the enemy without being seen, killing each one of them fast along with applying a great deal of fire power is what the ex-infantry soldier likes to do the best.

Hawk did several night operations in the Vietnamese war having great success in the south East Asian jungle using different stealth tactics.

His special forces training taught him how to sneak in on opposing targets without being seen is precisely what is soon to be applied out in the country side.

Once at the bushy over grown field in the rural farm land he parked at a handful of hours earlier Thomas slowly pulls off the gravel road killing the headlights.

The determined young man steadily cruises in through the wide open entrance that once had a swinging iron gate many years ago.

Semi blind Hawk drives his Impala into the open lot peering into the darkness that is on the other side of the windshield traveling to the tree line.

Cautiously Kevin turns the nineteen sixty five Chevrolet around backing a short distance into the wooded portion of the property.

He wants to be well prepared for a speedy departure from the site that is to be hit hard out in the desolation of rural northern Oregon.

There is a wide spot next to the two door Chevy for Sean to back in his full size four wheel drive truck. Armstrong follows suit having the Ford's head lights off in hope not to draw any unwanted attention from anybody off in the distance. The brown pickup is also well hidden from the view of would be passerby on Hemlock Road.

A quarter illuminated moon high above the earth on a cloudy night aids in making the environment darker. Having basically a moonless early December twilight is a huge plus for the small team of assassins.

Before getting out from behind the steering wheel of his metallic red Sedan, Kevin intently stares at his passenger with a serious look on his face. "I don't you to do something stupid that might get me or the other men killed. If I sense you are conducting yourself in a manner in our strike that may jeopardized any of our safety. I will put a bullet through your skull Kinsky!"

"I will do exactly as you tell me to do on the mission; chill out man I'm depending on you to lead me!"

"Those are the words to hear out of you Josh."

Upon stepping out from the driver's seat Hawk clearly begins hearing crickets as well as chirping birds far off from where he standing.

Surrounding tree branches rustle making audible crackling sounds from the strong blowing westward breeze. Sean along with his two cohorts is making as little noise as possible as they exit from the tall full size pick up. They quickly start to gear up in preparation for what's soon to come.

Armstrong takes the initiative as he climbs into the eight foot bed of his truck. Next he commences to hand out Nagely and Steele's rifles along with the necessary ammunition they'll be capping off.

Five determined men briskly walk single file the same path Thomas hiked upon earlier that day. Hawk has a red lens in his green military flashlight that gives off just enough illumination to see where he is stepping as he leads the squad.

At the tree line spot straight across from the gangs thought to be safe haven the suspended police officer rally's everyone around him. He goes over one last time how the surprise attack is to happen to give himself peace of mind.

Once Kevin is reassured that everybody is on the right page he has Alan get into his sniper position. Steele utilizes a low tree branch to steady his high powered rifle as he peers into the expensive magnifying scope with Hawk beside him gazing through his binoculars.

Sean and Clive hang tight while the pair carefully investigates the big old two story home two hundred meters away.

"Hey, Steele I'm staring at a lowlife in the dimly lit second story room that just stood up from the bed he was sitting on. It appears he has a rifle slung over his right shoulder!"

"I have him in my cross hairs Thomas; I am waiting for the guy to turn facing our direction." As was hoped for the man pivoted then strolled to the open upstairs window to perform the duty as a dependable watchman.

Gently Alan squeezed the trigger of the three hundred magnum rifle he firmly gripped in his strong hands. He fires the weapon in succession to the lookout sticking his head out of the open window for a better view of outside.

A nearly inaudible sound came from the high powered fire arm as it sends a high velocity thirty caliber bullet into the forehead of the unaware bad guy.

"Good shot Allen, that sent that fella right on his back where he belongs!" Declares Kevin as he peers through his binoculars at the two story building.

After Steele clears the way the first two men team of Sean and Clive swiftly exit the forest. The pair hurries toward the hideout in the tall grassy pasture while their SKS's are held at the ready position out in front of them.

Thomas goes back to peering to the farm's property as well as the first teams progress, "Ok, Kinsky let's make our way to the party! Make sure your weapon is locked and loaded safety off ready to shoot buddy!" Metallic clicks can be heard by Thomas as Josh flicks the switch to the fire position on the AK-47 he holds in front of him.

"I'm all set now Thomas!" Nervously the young street hustler informs in a very shaky voice a short distance from Hawk in the dusk. "Breathe in a deep hit of oxygen and follow me with your rifle trained not in my direction!" Thomas tells Kinsky prior to handing Steele his big bulky binoculars for safe keeping until he returns.

Allen wishes the pair good luck as they walked past him then cautiously made their way out of the thick foliage and onto the open clearing.

Kevin looked behind him motioning to Josh to stay crouched down as they hoof it across the grassy field. Hawk's heart is beating a little faster than usual from the anticipation of exterminating the murderous punks.

They double time it to a bushy blackberry briar area just on the other side of Hemlock Road taking a knee. Thomas takes a look across the short span to the hideout to make sure no gang members are visible.

All the first floor's thin old white curtains are closed and only the living room lights are on. He observes no one is outside of the residence.

"Hope your feet are set for a quick sprint my long haired friend, because we're heading to the front door in the quickness!"

"Let's get our groove on man!"

Instantly the big vigilante gets to his feet runs through a narrow opening of the blackberry thicket down across a shallow ditch.

In no time at all Hawk runs to the other side of the gravel road with Josh managing to stay a close distance behind the driven maniac.

Both men stay low as they quickly make their way over the tall wet lawn to the paint peeling wooden front steps. Quietly they each soft step it up to the entrance of the meth manufacture's home.

Not wasting any time Kevin kicks open the weathered wood door open with one powerful thrust kick. Lightning fast Thomas goes through the open doorway with the AK-47 aimed out in front of him.

A clearly shocked Stuart Thorne reaches for his blued double action pistol with the six inch barrel located on a sofa cushion on the husky thug's right.

Although the handgun is close to where he is seated on the maroon couch, his large hand barely touches the forty four magnum revolver. Hawk instantly has the jump on the Stranglehold leader filling his thick broad chest with thirty caliber rounds.

Lee Valentine a half Caucasian half Chinese Strangle Hold member is shot through the head. Kevin manages to short order the thin thug as he was standing from the sofa with a snub nose .38 pistol.

The skinny dope dealer shoots a bullet into the home's dirty wore out hardwood floor as he falls face first to the wood surface.

Kinsky is able to rapidly blast at the far side of the big open room, killing an Italian looking man with a handle bar style mustache.

The clean cut guy wearing a cheap brown leisure suit was attempting to aim an M-16 rifle in their direction as the pair entered the two story building.

He fell powerfully backward onto a dining room table breaking it onto the white linoleum, the bad guy twitched for a moment subsequent to death. Suddenly a barrage of gun fire takes them by complete surprise.

Josh doesn't know what hit him as he is shot multiple times in the chest and abdomen dropping him straight down upon his knees.

Slowly Kinsky went flat onto his chest, dead before he landed on the faded stained wooden surface that his feet seconds earlier stood strong upon.

A sneering Jimmy Bloodgood is rapidly laying down automatic fire from a nine millimeter sub machine gun out of the blue from an unlit hallway on the left.

Thomas performs a somersault rolling behind the long ripped up couch for a blocking barrier as he avoids taking a bullet. Promptly he returns shooting Bloodgood's way following hurrying to maneuver over the two street punk's lifeless bloody bodies.

The Strife leader ducks in and out of the hallway blasting away into the backside of the sofa as Hawk keeps low. Jimmy swiftly takes cover so he won't be shot by the popping up Thomas, who finds a window of opportunity to return fire in the thin doper's direction.

Loud deafening shots ring out in the in the large run down rural structure as the two men try their best to put an end to the other one's life.

A brief pause in the tumultuous fire fight happens when Kevin views the long straight haired drug dealer aim his weapon squeezing the trigger.

Only a metallic sound is to be made indicating the pale white male now possesses an empty gun. Hawk fires a fast three round burst at the under nourished career criminal who swiftly ducks out of sight.

The very quick moving Bloodgood has already dropped his automatic weapon in the hall then ran as fast as he could down the dark hallway.

"You lucky prick, next time I won't be missing when I have you in my sights!" Hawk said under his breath while slapping in another full magazine of rounds, locking and loading the AK 47 for more action.

Advancing in a rush the off duty police officer takes cover against the facing wall to his left. Thomas quickly peeks around the corner discovering a long dusky ominous hall that is vacant.

It contains two closed doors on the left side, one half gaped door on the opposite side along with a stairway at the end on the right.

Now in the silence he can hear rapid gun shots coming from off in the distance outside in the backyard portion of the property.

Kevin hurries past the peach color wallpaper riddled with bullets about head high on him. It was where the scum bag was standing as he attempted to snuff out the vengeful off duty law enforcement officer.

Crouching down on the move, the suspended cop briskly opens the wooden barriers that are on each side of the room finding no one inside.

In the last smaller room on the left just before the entrance to the staircase is a cluttered mess of duty antique furniture that reveals nothing as well.

Staying low Thomas cautiously makes his way toward the corner of the adjacent wall close to the beginning of the brown carpeted steps.

The stairs lead to the century old building's unheated second floor above.

Hot metal slug's whiz downward speeding into shadows at the tall vengeful man as he quickly peeks his head around the wall seeking Jimmy.

Hawk rapidly pivots back around away from the multitude of rounds race by his skull in the blink of an eye. Speeding bullets narrowly missed taking off his head before the muscular man took safe cover from the barrage of fire.

Kevin's back is flat to the peeling paper of the wall on the right side jam of the stairwell. His AK clutched tight to his thick chest trained toward the steps that are only a handful of inches away.

Gun powder lingers in the home's stuffy air from all the shooting that has transpired since the off duty officer entered the residence.

"Hey pig I have a friend who was upstairs sleeping when you rudely barged into our cozy home! Now I have a partner with me who wants you dead too man!"

Briefly Kevin peers back around glancing up at Jimmy as he loudly verbally chastises him in the semi darkness. A little light comes through the small round window high on the wall be behind the criminals.

He now observes through the shadows a much bigger guy standing on the right side of Bloodgood looking menacing as he holds a gun in his thick hand.

They are on the landing at the top of the first short flight of steps, prior to the staircase turning the corner continuing on to the second story above them.

Each thug has a nine millimeter pistol gripped firmly in their right hand. In a fast one eighty degree pivoting motion he's used several times as a Special Forces soldier in combat.

Hawk rolls out blasting the big thug square in the chest. The large heavy set punk falls forward tumbling down to the first floor hall.

Momentarily Hawk is forced to step out of the way of the bad guy who is falling down the steps. He still manages to shoot Bloodgood in the meaty portion of his hip before he flees up the remaining set of stairs.

Immediately the tall vigilante jumps over the stationary body to get to the beginning of the step. He chases after staying low as he hurries taking very brief cover positions as goes up to the second story.

Once at the top of the staircase Thomas pauses, listening intently prior to taking another step into the dusky narrow upstairs hall.

The upper level of the farm house is close to being completely pitch black; neither man dare turn on a light giving away his position.

Using full attention Kevin attempts to hear any kind of rustling, with no avail not a peep can be heard upstairs in the old site built structure.

Slow using a great deal of care Hawk proceeds forward stepping lightly on his size twelve combat boots on the hall's rickety floor.

Quietly he pushes open a closed door peering in through the shadows while staying off to the side of the square wood frame's opening.

Detecting no sign of Jimmy, only viewing the man Alan Steele took out of the equation lying flat on his back in the slightly moon lit room.

Thomas carefully continues down the inner second floor's inner corridor with the fully automatic rifle aimed ahead of him. His thick index finger gently touches the black metal trigger in anticipation of pulling back on it.

Abruptly a light thump noise comes from the inner wall of the bedroom a short distance away on the right. "The idiot is leaning against the wall in that room, I'm going to change that for the skinny dope head!" Kevin instantly thinks to himself as he trains his weapon in the direction of the adjacent wallpaper where the sound came from.

Without giving the street punk any warning Thomas rapidly fires a barrage of bullets into the framed barrier that separates the hallway from the end room.

Rushing down to the bedroom's entrance, Hawk instantly kicks open the thin door then quickly takes refuge away from the opening. Four rounds come through the wide open door frame striking the wall on the other side of dark hall.

A badly wounded Bloodgood is on the far side of the upstairs room shooting a handgun with one leg out of the window trying to escape.

Showing great skill along with speed, Hawk pops out firing high velocity slugs into the prostitute and drug peddling criminal that he can hardly believe is still alive.

Two of the full metal jacket rounds travel straight through his skull blowing out silver dollar size exit holes. The powerful impact sends Jimmy flying out of the second story window exhibiting great momentum.

His thin body tumbles a couple of hard times that making a lot of sound as he bounces off of the brittle cedar shingles of the front porch's decaying roof.

Advancing to the open window Thomas kneels down aiming through the sites of the Chinese AK-47 ready to lay down some more fire if need be.

Sprawled out on his belly is the now very dead Strife gang leader who put up a shockingly strong display of resistance toward the ex-Airborne Ranger.

"You murdered the wrong man's wife! Now you're going to burn in hell for what you've done piece of shit!" Hawk says under his breath in disbelief as he shakes his head about what just occurred.

CHAPTER 15 _____

Swift but remaining careful Kevin makes his way downstairs to where his fallen team mate is resting in the living room. He picks up the fully automatic rifle Josh was using, in one quick motion Thomas slings it over his broad shoulder.

Wasting no time Hawk regretfully positions Kinsky's body to make it appear as if he were part of the organization that just got shot up.

Ensuing closing the front door to give the home a normal appearance from gravel country road the suspended cop heads toward the kitchen.

He briskly strides through the first floor hurrying to get to the structure's back door to exit to the barn. Kevin is anxious to find out if everything went alright at the back of the property with team one's surprise attack.

Exiting from the old farmhouse's back screen door he sees from the eighty meter span under the barn's exterior light the huge red building's doors are open.

A one hundred watt bulb illuminates brightly from an exterior light mounted on a thick wood pole. Quickly he ambulates flanking wide to use the shadows of the Oak trees to the entrance of the good size structure.

Hawk scans side to side as he makes his way across the loose gravel attempting to view up ahead in the direction of the dimly lit hundred year old barn.

"Halt!! Who's there?" Armstrong yells out from the shadows just within the entrance of the huge farm building.

He is aiming his rifle at his team mate off in the distance not able to clearly make out the tall husky man's face as he comes to him.

"It's me Thomas! Hold your fire I'm coming up!"

"What are ya trying to do get yourself killed? Come on up crazy, I'm taking my finger off the trigger!" Sean replies stepping out with his SKS's barrel now pointed down at the gravel in front of him. "Where's the kid buddy?"

"He's dead inside the house!" Kevin says.

Approaching closer to Sean, Hawk observes Clive Nagely dragging a dead gang member inside the spacious structure to place it next to others.

The bearded big Ex-Green Beret is about to line up the corpse perfectly like the three others that are laying on their backs on the spread out blonde straw.

Their cotton T-shirts are currently saturated with dark red blood they will no longer need to sustain their lifeless bodies that are stiffening up.

"How many more do you have to put there Nagely? Thomas asked right before Clive dropped the low life's feet hard to onto the hay covered surface.

"Last one buddy, we ran out of turdballs to exterminate here on the ranch!" A pony tailed psycho declares upon turning to Hawk to look him in the eye.

"We're making it look like a contract hit so folks don't think this is a random accident or something." Armstrong says as he instinctually takes stock of what's around him as he stands right outside the barn.

"Are either of you hurt?"

"Neither of us got so much as a nick on us Thomas!"

"Yeah, me and Nagely got the jump on those punk kids! They were blindly shooting all over not knowing where to aim at!" Armstrong added.

"Very good fellas, come on let's get our asses out of here! I have places to go and people see gentlemen!" Hawk tells his fellow night assassins who have the mentality of still wanting a bit more action.

All three men double time it in the direction of where Alan Steele waits patiently with their automatic rifles slung across their backs.

Cold light precipitation starts coming down as they cross the large grassy field once again. It is a mixture of rain and hail that is steadily dropping from the black sky above.

Upon reaching the spot Steele plays the role of sniper Hawk keeps the chit chat to a bare minimum. He only allows a quick low down of what transpired at the Sauvie Island farm to be explained to Alan not wanting to waste needed time.

Subsequent to returning to their parked vehicles Sean and Kevin pull out onto the desolate country road having their headlights off. They hurry to cover up the tracks that were created by the tires in the lot's semi soft soil.

Each man either uses a square point shovel or metal rake that is removed from the eight foot bed of Armstrong's four wheel drive pickup truck.

Within minutes the war veterans hide the fact that a pair of automobiles drove upon the deserted old home stead property to the thick tree line.

"As I'm very positive that all of you have the same understanding that I do on what we did tonight. I still feel compelled to say, please tell absolutely no one of what we carried out here in the country side gentlemen!" Thomas states to the three behind the tailgate of his friend's big truck while it idles facing to the north.

"Heck I am taking this adventure to my grave guys!" Alan states as he glances to each of them displaying sincerity in his eyes as he spoke.

"Same goes for me boys! I like having my freedom, this ever leaks out we'll all be behind bars!" Clive added appearing serious. Sean silently nodded in agreement in what was being expressed openly.

"Outstanding gentlemen, I can't thank you enough for helping me rid society of those pieces of garbage."

"Thomas believe me, it was truly our pleasure to do it. If we don't high tail it out of here soon, we're liable to be seen by a country bumpkin cruising in his truck out poaching deer or something!" Armstrong said then took a step toward Hawk shaking his hand.

Each man shook Kevin's hand as they told the stocky man good bye and wished him well. As the Ford pickup motors off into the darkness carrying away the crew of vigilantes Thomas changes back into casual street attire.

He keeps an eye out for head lights looking into the cold black night air while quickly putting on his clothing by the Chevy's open unlit trunk.

While driving back to Portland on Sauvie Island's rural roads with the radio's volume fairly low the suspended police officer has the sensation of deep satisfaction.

Though Kevin doesn't feel that he handled his wife's killers morally in the right manner, it was the only way he could have possibly live with.

Having piece of mind Thomas listens to rock and roll songs that a local radio channel plays having very little interruptions from commercials.

He sees just one other motorist that is traveling in the opposite direction in the farm country many miles from where his hit took place earlier.

At the Portland International Airport's parking garage Hawk takes a two hour power nap in his vehicle with the black vinyl bucket seat reclined back.

A refreshed Kevin Thomas awakes a little past at three am Thursday morning forgetting where he was from the deep sleep.

In the airport, Kevin makes his way through a short line where a courteous African American lady working for the airline is using promptly validates a four thirty departure plane ticket to South Vietnam.

One of the male suitcase handlers checking in bags puts paper destination sticker tags on each of Hawk's pieces of luggage.

Following the necessary flight arrangements, Kevin promptly strides to one of the airports restrooms to take care of some needed personal hygiene.

He washes his face in the stainless steel sink prior to a lathery shave to remove the thick black stubble. Kevin really didn't want Linn's relatives to lay their eyes upon a homeless looking man when he shows up at the small village they live in.

Air World Airline's Flight 74 departure to the South Vietnam Airport of Ho Chi Minh City International takes off a little over a half an hour late.

The plane ride seemed longer than he remembered from years earlier. Touching down on the foreign country's tarmac is extremely welcomed by Thomas.

His long legs have been cramped against the seat in front of him for many hours high in the Earth's stratosphere. Former city once called Saigon, now known as Ho Chi Minh City is basically as the Ex-Airborne Ranger remembers.

At his mother in laws small rural village north of the city Kevin is welcomed with great love. He gives his spouse's possessions to her elderly mom who looks like the old version of Linn.

The week and a half he shares with his wife's hospitable loved ones is very cathartic for emotionally hurting man. Sharing stories along with pictures of young South Vietnamese woman touched his heart in a positive way.

It felt pretty good to Hawk to speak Vietnamese again on a daily basis with the kind much shorter than himself South East Asian people.

At first the language came out of Kevin's mouth a bit slower along with miss pronouncing some words. In no time at all he was back fluently caring on conversations with everybody around him.

Linn's ashes arrived toward the end Thomas's stay with the tight community in the dark green rain forest countryside delivered by a small postal van.

Her small stainless steel urn is tightly packaged in a brown cardboard box that is stuffed with pink bubble wrap for safe keeping.

There is a long condolence letter from Kevin's parents along with a few cards from Linn's customers which he read to the Vietnamese family.

A formal ceremony was organized with everyone dressing in their best clothes. Even though there were tears flowing at times it was more of a celebration of what was once a beautiful young lady very full of life.

Linn's younger sister Hani Huong helps Kevin spread the ashes along the small pond she grew up fishing and swimming in.

A feast of food ended on a long out door table where a couple dozen hungry people sat at to partake in grubbing on the delicious bounty.

Leaving to catch the beat up taxi cab that has arrived to drive Hawk back to the airport there was a lot of crying as well as long embraces.

The petite small emotional Vietnamese in laws took turns coming to Thomas hugging him and expressing their feelings as they sincerely thanked him for coming.

Epilogue _____

Back in Portland Oregon, Sergeant Thomas is formally investigated by his Northeast police department due to anonymous phone calls. Hawk had a hunch that the callers were the remaining cowardly law breaking Strife and Strangle Hold members.

The 341st NE precinct detectives checks Kevin out with a fine tooth comb after serving with a judge granted search warrant. His home is thoroughly checked out top to bottom as it searched for firearms that may link him to the Sauvie Island massacre.

Phone records of recent calls made from the suspected police officer's home are looked over. Not an incriminating clue turns up during the privacy invading inspection that took several weeks to complete.

Kevin is given letter of apology from Chief of Police Duane Blythe as well as being fully reinstated as a Portland police officer in the NE precinct.

The inquisition doesn't get Hawk down; it spurred him on to becoming a homicide detective to rid society of those who murder the weaker.

In succession to his house selling for modest price, Thomas moves into a one bedroom apartment close to the community college he enrolls in.

He utilizes a large portion of his funds taking courses on forensic medicine and criminal investigation in the evenings as well as on weekends.

After two years of studying advanced criminology, Kevin Thomas is transferred where he is needed as a homicide detective.

He makes his home at Seattle's 893 Westside precinct 234th Division where he is given his own small office to work out of on the third floor.

While solving a late neighborhood drive by shooting at his downtown high rise police station Detective Thomas meets an attorney named Arianna Mancini.

The tan skinned woman with the long wavy brunette hair strolled into his office one afternoon looking for the station's Captain.

Kevin and Arianna slowly began dating as time allowed in their hectic schedules in the busy northwest city of Seattle Washington.